SHOW NO MERCY

A STEVE DANE THRILLER

BRIAN DRAKE

WOLFPACK
PUBLISHING
— EST 2013 —

Show No Mercy

Paperback Edition
Copyright © 2020 Brian Drake

Wolfpack Publishing
5130 S. Fort Apache Road, 215-380
Las Vegas, NV 89148

wolfpackpublishing.com

Paperback ISBN 978-1-64734-233-3
eBook ISBN 978-1-64734-231-9

SHOW NO MERCY

CHAPTER 1

——■——

Steve Dane wasn't afraid of heights but being on the thirtieth floor of the high rise over downtown San Francisco made him wonder. The wind rattled the window pane and the quiver in his stomach could not be denied. Despite the glass, he felt like the wind could sweep him into space at any second.

When the double-doors opened behind him, Dane gratefully turned from the window.

Ray Lucas, Dane's potential client, entered. He wore a dark suit not unlike Dane's, an obvious custom fit, his tie a little askew and worry-lines on his 60-plus-year-old face. Lucas closed the door behind him and joined Dane at the window. "Incredible view, isn't it? During Fleet Week you get a perfect look at the aircraft carriers. The Blue Angels fly right by."

The people on the street below might as well have been ants. Vehicles looked like toys, but the view beyond impressed Dane indeed.

The Bay Bridge stretched across the water, connecting to the flat Treasure Island and rocky Yerba Buena Island in the distance. Under the bridge, huge tankers and smaller boats moved along the water, the boats with high full-blooming sails taking the most advantage of the windy day and going faster than their motorized counterparts.

"Let's have a seat," Lucas said.

Lucas led Dane across to the solid oak conference table on the other side of the room. The seat cushion let out a hiss of air as Dane sat. Lucas removed a smart phone from inside his jacket.

"You come highly recommended," Lucas said.

"I was told," Dane said, "that your issue was a personal matter. That's a little out of my area of expertise."

"No, this is definitely your kind of job. I need somebody who can shoot his way out, if necessary, because I think it *will* be necessary."

Steve Dane certainly fit the bill if a job required shooting. Former CIA, former Marine, former mercenary commander. He'd seen the world at its best and worst; from the most affluent areas of Europe and the US, to the sun-soaked sands of the African desert to, sometimes, even harsher environments. Always with a weapon, always with the goal of fighting for the underdog who had no champion.

And he did it all with the help of the love of his life, Nina Talikova, herself a former Russian agent who had joined his crusade.

"Tell me about it," Dane said. He was dressed similarly to Lucas, though his suit had come from Savile Row and the silver cuff-links were real. The mix of laugh lines and frown lines on his face hinted at a wide variety of experience. If Lucas saw Dane tug on the right cuff of his jacket, he made no mention. It was an absent-minded habit for Dane, but he had a reason.

With nervous fingers, Lucas tapped the screen of his phone and showed the display to Dane. A picture of a girl. Red hair, flower-print sundress, bright smile. "My daughter, Brenda."

Lucas leaned forward. "Brenda's twenty-two years old. Bit of a wild child. I suppose that's what I get for working as much as I have with a wife who wasn't necessarily up for the job of raising children. Brenda's been on her own a lot, but she's never been in any serious trouble until now. A few weeks ago, she received pictures in the mail. They show her in some rather, um, compromising positions."

"Blackmail?"

"My family is not unknown in this city. It may be a small pond, but we're some of the larger fish. The release of those pictures would cause a scandal, hurt my family *and* my business."

Dane waited for more and watched a worried look flash across Lucas's face. He kept up an unflappable front, but Dane could see the pain behind his eyes.

"I hired a private investigator to track down the man responsible." A swipe on the screen revealed another face, an older man with a touch of gray in his dark hair. "This is Terry Park. Man-about-town with no visible means of support, as the police might say. My detective says he's a professional blackmailer. He's put the bite on thousands of people, all around the country. Used to work out of Los Angeles, mostly. But now he's here."

"Your man can't do anything?"

"My man *won't* do anything. Nothing illegal."

"Have you negotiated to buy the pictures?"

"I won't pay extortion money, Mr. Dane. I want the pictures. I want you to steal them."

"Fair enough."

"Can you do that?"

"You've left out a few details. Like where I can find

him. Where is he hiding the photographs?"

Lucas nodded and put away the phone. "Forgive me, I'm. . ."

"It's okay."

"He has a house in Marin County, near the Golden Gate Bridge. Top of a hill. I have the address. It's a rental, one of the hundreds of McMansions you can get around here. He's throwing a party tomorrow night. My detective has determined the pictures are on a computer in his office. I have the passwords for the computer."

"You have everything except somebody willing to do the job."

"Yes."

"How do you know your detective is correct?"

"Well. . ."

"He has somebody on the inside?"

Lucas swallowed. "Park has a girlfriend who wants out. I paid her for the information."

"And if she's lying?"

"Mr. Dane. . ."

"Why can't she get the pictures?"

"I asked. He'll want her beside him during the party. The best she can do is keep him occupied. And provide a key to his office."

"Why should I expect shooting?"

Lucas regained his composure. "Park has armed guards all over the house. He always travels with at least one in public."

"How many?"

Lucas blanched. "I don't know."

"You're aware of my fee?" Dane said.

"A million bucks to me is like fifty cents to somebody else, Mr. Dane. I'm willing to pay more."

"That's all right. But I have to tell you I may be walking into a complete mess. You don't know the number of guards and Park's girlfriend may be a fink. I've turned down jobs for less."

"Please—"

Dane held up a hand. "I'll do it. If I fail, you won't owe me anything."

"Fail?"

"With what you've told me about this place, it's a reasonable possibility."

Lucas put his phone away. His hands were shaking. "I could use a drink," he said. "Would you like one?"

"Here at the office?"

"Good heavens, no, there's a very nice bar across the street. We have to go out the back way otherwise my secretary will tell my wife I went there."

Dane smiled and rose with Lucas. "I never say no to a drink."

Lucas smiled as well. His smile showed a change in his demeanor. He was now a man encouraged everything was going to be okay. But Dane wasn't so sure. He wouldn't be sure until he had the pictures.

CHAPTER 2

———■———

The rain had stopped hours ago and the streets were slick with condensation resembling sweat. Not even Hans Mueller's long coat blocked the four a.m. chill off Berlin's Spree River.

The German bomb expert stood over five feet high. The long black coat stopped around his ankles and a knit cap rode atop his head. His pale lips and lack of eyebrows were his most distinguishing features, and his eyes picked out almost every detail around him.

He leaned against the wall of an alcove at the corner of Poststrabe and Rathaustrabe, among darkened cafe fronts. The ghost-like buildings were eerily silent. Across from him, a construction zone, half-walls and silent cranes and other equipment waiting for daylight. A few stray cars lined the curbs on either end of the street, but no others traveled the roadway at this hour. The river whispered nearby.

Hans Mueller stood with his hands jammed deep into the pockets of his coat, the right pocket bulging a little more because of the pistol he held in his hand. He had arranged the meeting at this location but he also knew the rendezvous might be a trap. If they were coming to get him, he'd go down fighting. Such a day had to come eventually.

A long black car turned the corner up ahead. Its bright headlights flashed across the construction site and caused a glare on the wet pavement. When the lights hit Mueller with the ferocity of a stage spotlight, he couldn't help but raise his left hand to block the light and pull his Glock with the other. There was a round in the chamber. His finger rested on the trigger.

The black car stopped a few feet away, a Mercedes-Benz S600 limousine, black with silver trim. The headlamps burned brightly. Those same lights flashed twice, stayed off, turned on again and flashed twice more. Mueller put the Glock away. The rear door opened when he approached the car. The figure inside, briefly visible as the interior light spilled onto the sidewalk, slid back as Mueller ducked to enter.

"You are the last person I expected to see in this car," Mueller said as he sat. The man across from him cracked a polished smile.

"Yet here I am," said Mason Graypoole.

The bench seats faced each other. On Graypoole's side, he had a rotating flat screen connected to a laptop.

Track lighting in the roof lit the cabin brightly. There was almost no sense of movement with the lighting and tinted windows. The soundproofing muted the engine noise to dull throb. The warmth of the cabin and its soft leather seats might have been a womb.

Mueller regarded Mason Graypoole curiously. He looked better than the last time Mueller had seem him. The man had always been tubby, a testament to his lifestyle of all-party-no-work, but now he was lean and trim, with a sharp line to his jaw and the obvious custom suit fitted him well. "What are you doing here?"

"We're going to finish my father's work," Graypoole said.

"I don't believe you. Your father always spoke of you as a secret weapon, but all we saw was a drunken leech who partied away his money."

"Not all of it." Graypoole grinned.

A hot flush crept up Mueller's neck. "If this is supposed to be some sort of. . .whatever you call it, all you're doing is pissing me off."

Graypoole held up a hand. "You're right. I was everything you accuse me of. Since my mother died, I've been doing some soul-searching. Read my father's papers, his manifesto. I used a phony name and joined a mercenary group. Fought in Africa, Eastern Europe, learned the tricks of the trade and how to face down an enemy, all in preparation for my plans. I even became an expert at hapkido. In other words, I've had a change of heart. Now the least I can do to pay my father back is to carry on the fight, and we'll start by avenging his murder."

"I'm still not convinced, but try and impress me."

"Here's what we're doing." Graypoole turned the flat screen toward Mueller and started pressing buttons on the keyboard. "I need a man to blow up a part of San Francisco." An image of the city, the Bay Bridge specifically, appeared on the screen. "Go there and pick a target."

Mueller nodded. "Budget?"

"No expense spared. Bring some friends, if you'd like. I want mass casualties. Total chaos."

"Why San Francisco?"

"Why not? The city is the growing home to many tech companies, many big shot CEOs, many others who are working on new inventions in their garage in order to join those ranks. It's the kind of target my father could not have overlooked. And, besides, we need to give New York and Los Angeles a break. Somebody is always blowing up those cities. We need to be original."

Graypoole grinned at his joke but Mueller didn't laugh. The assassination of Mason's father had driven their organization so far underground Mueller didn't think they'd ever recover. Each and every one of them had a target on their back. Mason may have had the primary reason for wanting revenge, but it was something they all craved, too. And here was an opportunity Mueller couldn't resist.

"When should I start?" the German said.

"Right now."

Graypoole lifted a handset from door panel on his right and spoke to the driver. The car made a long turn and straightened out. After the turn, there was once again only a small sense of forward movement when the engine surged.

Presently the Mercedes slowed and swung curbside. Graypoole pulled a small notebook from inside his coat, along with a pen, and scribbled briefly. He tore the page out and handed it to Mueller, who examined the words, and handed it back. Graypoole crumpled the paper and extended his hand. "Much success. You're the first salvo."

"Who's the second?"

"Ramos."

Mueller let a smile pull at the corners of his mouth. He exited back into the cold of the early Berlin morning. The Mercedes drove away as his shoes tapped a rhythm on the concrete and he felt warm all over. If the car had been a womb, he was now reborn.

He'd entered the limo a hermit and emerged a warrior.

CHAPTER 3

——■———

Steve Dane surveyed the party. He leaned against the bar, holding a martini in his right hand. He wore a tux like the rest of the men and the women decked out in a variety of gowns and party dresses. Their jewelry was no match for the gems in the four chandeliers hanging from the ceiling, but not many noticed. The party had been in full swing for two hours. Dane's invitation had been provided by Park's girlfriend and nobody had second-guessed his presence. So far, she was the perfect insider.

Dane's tux had been specially tailored for the event. Instead of his usual shoulder harness with .45 auto, he wore a harness containing rappelling spikes. Cummerbund concealed a nylon rope. A few other goodies rode in pockets. His exit strategy did not include the front door.

The dark-haired host, Terry Park, his tux accentuated with a red bow tie, approached the bar, his red-haired girlfriend on his arm. In her heels, she was two inches taller. She wore a tight blue party dress with a plunging neckline. Dane wondered where she'd put the key.

Park ordered a Maker's Mark on the rocks. Another

man at the bar said hello. As Park turned to engage, Dane and the redhead exchanged nods. While Park and the bartender exchanged a little sports talk, she slipped a thumb and finger between her breasts and retrieved a small item which she placed underneath a stray napkin. Park took his Maker's Mark and he departed with the redhead in tow. They continued to mingle as guests either danced or conversed at tables.

Dane downed his martini and asked for a refill. The bartender turned his back, and Dane swept the napkin over. The key dropped into a pocket.

The singer-and-piano combo on a raised platform in the corner kept the music going, the young women in sequined blue currently in the middle of an up-tempo number. Dane absently tapped his foot, his mind on what waited for him upstairs.

The armed guards Park kept at his McMansion weren't evident in the ballroom. They were spread out around the property and probably upstairs too.

Great. The job was never easy.

Dane finished the second martini and placed the glass on the bar.

He strolled along the wall and slipped through a doorway. Signs pointed to restrooms with a branching hall blocked by a velvet rope. Dane stepped over the rope and continued down a dark hall leading to the main entryway. Staircase ahead. Dane went up the stairs and unbuttoned his jacket. He stopped at the second-floor landing.

"You're not allowed up here."

The tuxedoed guard had a chrome dome and goatee sprinkled with gray. The tux did not conceal his bulky chest or the pistol under his right arm.

"Go back."

Dane kicked the guard in the groin. The big man let out a small squeal, the steel toes in Dane's shoe delivering the desired effect. Dane swung a right into the man's jaw and the guard went down for the count. Dane stepped over the man to open a nearby closet and grabbed the guard under the arms. He pulled and grunted, straining like he was moving a couch. Dane dragged the man into the closet and shut him in. He leaned against the wall a moment to catch his breath. He hoped there weren't any others.

Dane continued down the hall. No lights. He felt along the wall until he came to a set of double doors. He tried the knob because sometimes people left doors unlocked. Not in this case. He took out the key. The lock snapped back. Dane opened the door, went inside and turned the lock behind him.

He left the lights off and used the cell to light his way to Park's desk, eyeing the curtained window close by. Hello, exit. He eased behind the desk. A keyboard and monitor sat on the desktop, the screen blank. A tap of a key brought the screen back to life. A box in the center prompted him for a password.

Dane took a folded piece of paper from his shirt pocket and typed the password with one finger. As he moved the finger to the enter key, he hoped the girlfriend hadn't forgotten a character. He pressed the button and the screen cleared. Bingo.

Dane consulted the paper again and selected the needed file folder. The thumb drive from another pocket went into the USB port on the box under the desk. Dane dumped the files onto the thumb drive. The status bar made a slow crawl from left to right.

Dane glanced at the office door. Still closed.

He pulled back the drapes and unlatched the window.

Raising it all the way, he started to detach the screen. Cold air rushed in. Sweat trickled down his neck and the shirt stuck to his back despite the cooling breeze.

Dane placed the window screen on the carpet and returned to the desk. The status bar showed 30%.

He glanced at the door again.

The cummerbund slipped off quickly and Dane uncoiled the rope from around his waist. He removed a spike from under his left arm and looped the rope through. He slammed the spike into the wall below the window. Laughter drifted up from below. Female voices. More laughing.

Dane returned to the desk, his pulse quickening. 52%. Come on! Another look at the door. He should have taken the guard's gun, but one of his goals was to avoid shooting, despite what Lucas said. The last thing he wanted was a fight with a ton of civilians in the way.

56%.

If Park had a Mac, Dane would be gone by now.

He tapped a beat on the desk. He looked around. One wall was lined with books; a map of the world on the opposite wall. Push pins in the map probably identified places where Park had operated, or where police interest made him no longer welcome.

Finally, the status bar cleared and Dane pulled out the thumb drive. He returned it to the pocket from whence it came. Then he clicked on the Lucas folder, as well as others, and dragged them to the trash. He deleted the trashed items.

Then keys rattled the lock and the knob turned.

CHAPTER 4

━━■━━■━━

Dane raced to the window and grabbed the rope. The door swung open. Dane couldn't make out the face of the man entering, but the new arrival said, "Hey!" and clawed under his coat.

The lights snapped on and Dane winced at the sudden brightness, swinging one leg out, then the other, bracing both feet against the outer wall. He quick-stepped down the wall. Dane dropped into the yard and flashed a smile at the trio of sloshed women as he ran to the wall across the yard. Their chatter stopped and they stared at him.

As he ran, he heard the voice of the man in the window yelling into a radio.

Dane scaled the wall, tearing his pants as he rolled over the top. The ground below was not only soft but sloped. He landed wrong and fell, jumping up to run down the slope, dodging trees, the low branches stabbing at him.

Park's troops would be quietly mobilizing for pursuit.

Dane tripped on a fallen branch and fell headlong into the dirt. Winded, he spat dirt from his mouth and started again. Getting killed by Mother Nature wasn't on his bucket list.

He cleared the forest and reached a road. A car waited fifteen yards ahead. Dane completed the dash in seconds.

The car was a rental, a generic white Chevrolet Impala and the engine fired. The lights snapped on as Dane approached. He dropped into the passenger seat. The woman behind the wheel wrapped slender pink-tipped fingers around the gear lever and pulled it into Drive.

"Success?" she said in her Russian-dusted accent.

"I tore my pants."

"Did the baddies see your boxers?"

"I think we're okay."

"The photos?"

"I got them, honey."

The glow of the dash highlighted Nina Talikova's smile. Her face sparkled. She was the love of Dane's life. Muscles in her forearms flexed as he gripped the wheel and followed the twisting road. She wasn't dressed for a party, wearing jeans with running shoes and a blue tank top.

"Company coming," she said.

"How many?"

"Looks like one car with its high-beams on."

"Typical."

Dane reached under the seat and pulled out a small box. He extracted a stainless-steel Detonics Scoremaster .45 auto, recently rebuilt with new internal parts since Dane used the weapon as much as he did. His gunsmith had suggested an upgrade to an entirely new gun, but Dane refused. The gun let out a loud *chuh-chink* as he chambered a round.

Nina braked for a sharp turn and accelerated out of it.

"They're gaining."

"They know this road better than you," he said.

"I'll manage, honey," she said. Then: "Mind your head."

Gunfire crackled behind them and the bullets smacked the Impala's body. Dane rolled onto the back seat and powered down the passenger window. Another shot nicked the rear window and left a spider-crack behind.

Dane leaned out and fired twice in return. The enemy car swerved across the opposite lane and Dane crossed to the other window. Another shot shattered the rear window entirely. Shards of glass peppered Dane. He leaned out but lurched to one side as Nina took another sharp turn. The road straightened once again. Dane fired as the enemy car cleared the corner. Nina pressed on the accelerator and the Impala surged ahead, putting significant distance between them and the other car. A muzzle flash winked and one of the rear tires exploded, bits of hot rubber pelting Dane in the face. The car fishtailed as the steel rim shrieked on the asphalt. The force of the fishtail jammed Dane against one side of the window frame and he almost lost his grip on the .45. Nina slowed the car and pulled off the road.

"I hope you brought a bazooka," Dane said. He and Nina scrambled out and took cover at the front of the car.

Nina drew a Smith & Wesson M&P Shield from a holster behind her back. Her pink fingernails clashed with the flat black of the pistol's frame.

"The gun shop was smack out of bazookas. I put my name on a waiting list, though."

"Good thinking." Dane slammed a ten-round extended magazine into the Scoremaster. The enemy car skidded to a stop perpendicular to them. They started to rise when somebody stuck a machine pistol out the side window. Dane and Nina dropped as the full-auto burst raked the

Impala. Two gunners jumped out of the car during the blast. Dane fired and one of the shooters let out a scream.

Dane and Nina zeroed on the side window as the machine pistol fell silent. Their handguns cracked in quick succession. The rounds scored. The gunner in the car fell back, his weapon clattering on the ground.

Dane and Nina reloaded. The feet of the last gunner shuffled under the car.

"Stay put," Dane said. He scooted around the side of the Impala, crawling along the dirt shoulder. He reached the back tire and stayed flat.

The last gunner peeked over the hood and fired at Nina. She returned the shot. Dane fired once. The top of the last gunner's head exploded in a sheet of red. He fell back with a thud.

The echo of the shots faded. Dane and Nina waited. When no further threats emerged, Dane rose and went back to Nina.

"You're a mess," she said.

Dane's tux was not only torn but covered with bits of glass and road grime. He tucked away his gun, opened the driver's side door and popped the trunk.

"The car is a mess too," Nina said.

"Hopefully the spare isn't damaged."

Dane lifted the trunk and handed her the jack stand and unlatched the spare from its hold.

Nina raised an eyebrow. "Did you sign for the extra insurance?"

Dane turned off the shower. It was well past three a.m. but he was still keyed up from the night's action.

The rush was always stimulating, but Dane carried

scars to remind him someday the "rush" might be the end of him. He started to dry off. The worst of the damage was along his right arm and part of his chest, the flesh puckered and warped. During his days as a CIA agent, on a mission in Central America specifically, his Blackhawk had crashed. As he and others pulled the injured from the wreckage, leaking gas splashed on Dane, then part of the chopper exploded. The flames lit him up like a candle. He rolled in the dirt, others assisting to put out the flames, but the damage had been done. His team had to carry him through the jungle for two days before they arranged extraction, then he spent the next six months in a hospital. It could have been worse, but the scarring reminded him while he had survived the worst, he was not invincible.

He carried other scars, too, not visible. He'd seen a lot of victories, but also his share of defeats. Friends had been killed supporting his efforts. Some of the violence hit close to home too.

But he'd survived. The scars and tragedy had not stopped him from living life to the full, to the very edge. A lot of guys weren't as fortunate as he.

Dane later cut loose from the CIA to form his own mercenary unit, the 30-30 Battalion. It was an opportunity to take charge of his life and forge his own destiny. A skirmish in South Africa netted him controlling interest in a diamond mine and he disbanded the unit. He was still for hire, but also found time to fight for those who couldn't afford his fee. He enjoyed bringing a fight to the predators who sought to exploit the defenseless. Idealistic, yes. He could afford to be idealistic.

Dane pulled on a robe and dropped the towel in the corner.

He found her sitting up in bed, a glass of chilled vodka in hand. Her hair was tied up, stray strands falling alongside her slender neck. Nina had once been a highly decorated agent with the Russian FSB. She and Dane met when Dane was in Europe investigating the possibility that a pair of Anastasia's jewels had showed up on the underground market. The "possibility" had been a ruse, the jewels nothing but a pair of really good fakes, but as Dane sought the items for his own profit and Nina for her country's history, their genuine chemistry assured both they would soon pledge all of their remaining days to each other.

They occupied a top floor two-room suite at the Hyatt near the Embarcadero. The bedroom was smaller than Dane would have liked, but the larger living room had a huge 60-inch screen mounted on the wall. All the comforts of home, plus room service.

Dane picked up his cell phone from the dresser and called a number. The call went to voicemail. No normal people were up this late.

"It's Dane. We have the pictures. We'll meet you tomorrow at one at the mall, Market Street entrance."

Dane put down the phone.

"Couldn't wait till morning?" Nina said.

"I'd have been thinking about it the rest of the night."

She finished her drink and put the empty glass on the nightstand. "Help me up."

He put some force behind the pull and she yelped as her body slammed into his. Her arms snaked around his neck. He undid her robe and drew his hands along the curves of her hips, up her back, pulling her closer. Her bare skin was not only soft but hot to the touch. He leaned down to kiss along the edge of her neck. Her shoulders tensed and she let out a gasp.

"Your stubble tickles."

"Mmmm-hmmmm."

"It's time for bed," she said.

"If you say so."

She dragged her fingernails down his back. "I say so."

CHAPTER 5

━━◆━━

Time to get paid.

They had to take a cab to the Westfield Shopping Center on Market Street, as the rented Chevy was abandoned in an alley off Battery. Dane wasn't worried about fallout with the Impala. He'd signed for the car under an alias matching the name on his passport, driver's license, and MasterCard.

Traffic barely moved. Pedestrians walked faster than the cars rolled. The tall steel-and-glass buildings up and down the street blocked the sun, and there was a chill in the shade.

Dane paid the cabbie and he and Nina found a bench in the shade of the mall's entrance. He wore his usual dark suit, white shirt, with a red tie. Usually only the color of the tie changed. Black shoes, polished, steel-toed. Pistol under his left arm, the jacket tailored with extra space so the gun didn't show.

Nina looked terrific as usual in a green skirt and black top with flats, her hair cascading down her back and shoulders. She wore a small purse cross-body. Inside the purse was her S&W pistol.

Even at noon, the place was busy. Shoppers went in with nothing and exited loaded with bags to join the massive flow of people on the sidewalks. More shops waited, along with a smattering of restaurants, some with sidewalk seating. Homeless sitting up against the wall were for the most part ignored; there were a lot of them up and down the street, some stretched out over sidewalk grates where warm air from the underground transit system wafted.

Dane removed a cigar tube from the inside pocket of his jacket and extracted a Montecristo. He lit the foot with a Vector triple-torch lighter and took a few puffs.

Nina yawned.

"Long night?"

She punched him in the arm. There was a soda machine near the entrance. Nina went over to it and returned with a bottle of Coke.

"I can't wait till we get home," she said. "No more jobs the rest of the year."

"You'll get bored within a week and start bugging me to find work."

Her gaze lingered on the variety of activity around them, the passing people, the cars and the construction down the block.

"This place is one extreme or the other," she said.

Dane puffed his cigar. A passing woman in a tan overcoat gave him a dirty look.

"What do you mean?"

"The smoke Nazi bitch for one," Nina said. "You have the tourists ogling everything like they've never seen a chain store before. Over there the Wall Street-types who live in another city, probably. The girl over there with the green hair and oh my God those pants. Looks like her girlfriend vomited on her. Walks right by the Brooks

Brothers and they don't even bat an eye."

"It's eclectic."

"It's strange."

Dane shrugged.

"Come on, you know I'm right. We're in a nicer spot, too. Go over a block and the homeless crap on the sidewalk."

"Shall we?"

"Not in these shoes," she said.

Dane let out another stream of smoke. "You have a point, but as somebody once said, I wouldn't squeeze it too hard. It's the way it is here. A lot of people like it. Not every city can be Paris."

"*Paris* isn't even Paris anymore."

"We won't be here much longer."

"I'd rather be in Nicaragua up to my tits in leeches."

"That I'd like to see."

She jabbed him in the belly with a stiff finger, the sharp nail digging into his skin.

"Ouch," he said.

"Serves you right." She took another drink of her Coke.

Ray Lucas broke from the flow and removed a pair of aviator sunglasses. He held a tablet computer in his left hand. He and Dane shook hands.

"Nina, this is Ray Lucas, the client."

She yawned again before shaking hands. "A thousand pardons, late night."

"So I hear," Lucas said. "Our connection said . . . well, she mentioned a thing or two. Park is clearing out."

"And the girlfriend?"

"Not my concern."

"I was wrong about her," Dane said. "The information provided was 100% accurate." Dane held the Montecristo in the right corner of his mouth while he took out the thumb drive. Lucas plugged it into a tablet computer and scanned the contents of the folder.

"Okay," Lucas said. He traded the tablet for a smart phone and Dane produced his own phone. A few screen taps later and the million-dollar fee was electronically transferred to Dane's Swiss account.

"Thank you, Mr. Dane." Lucas shook his hand again.

"I was there, too," Nina said.

"I appreciate your effort, ma'am."

Lucas donned his aviators and walked away.

"Shall we do some shopping?" Dane said.

"I'd rather go back to bed."

Dane started to reply when an explosion rocked the mall.

The ground seemed to rise and drop again with a violent jolt and knocked Dane and Nina off balance. Dane forced her to the ground. The Coke bottle and cigar went flying. Dane stayed on top of Nina for a moment. The ground shook again with another blast and smoke drifted skyward from the roof of the mall.

The doors crashed open. People ran out screaming and when automatic weapons began popping. Dane rolled of Nina.

"We should get out of here," she said.

"I'll meet you back at the hotel." Dane took out his gun.

"Steve—"

"Go if you want!"

Dane charged forward, his face a mask of concentration, but he didn't look back. He knew Nina was behind him.

They plowed through the panicked shoppers and ran inside. The mall was two stories. Straight ahead was the upper walkway with a railing overlooking the bottom floor.

The automatic weapons echoed through the mall, the noise mixing with screams. Bodies riddled with bullets already lined the walkway, some with loved ones wailing over them. Smoke and dust filled the air. The blast had sucked out most of the oxygen and it was hard to breathe. Victims covered with blood and dust staggered in a daze.

Dane and Nina ran to the nearest victims, coaxing them to their feet and shoving them toward the exit with encouraging words about their loved ones. Dane grabbed a young woman by the shoulders and pulled her away from a fallen older male.

"No! That's my father!"

"I'll get him but you gotta get out of here!"

Men with AKM automatic rifles emerged from the front of a store to the left. They raised their weapons. Dane shouted for her to get down, trying to push her in such a way as to shield her body, but she continued to struggle against him and the AKM muzzles flashed. The girl slammed into Dane's chest as the 7.62x39 slugs smacked into her, her pleading eyes, big, brown and wide, on his, the flash of pain brief across her face as the gunmen's slugs tore her apart. Both of them fell, Dane landing on his back with the girl's dead body atop him. Her blood leaked onto his shirt. Nina screamed something. Dane rolled the girl of him and jumped to his feet with the Detonics .45 outstretched.

CHAPTER 6

━━━━━━━━━■━━━━━━━━━

Dane's first shot split open the head of one shooter. Blood and bone sprayed from his skull onto his partner, who snapped his head around. Before the second shooter brought around his AKM, two 9mm stingers from Nina's S&W blasted out one eye and his two front teeth.

Dane shot the third gunner, who died with his finger on the trigger. As he fell, the AKM swung up and hosed, bits of debris falling from the ceiling.

Screams continued to echo.

More shooting from the lower level. Nina ran forward and Dane rotated 360 degrees to check their back side before running after her.

They'd be counted among the enemy when the cops arrived.

But the ghosts of battles past urged Dane on. The pleading eyes of the dead girl forced him to continue.

The mall stretched ahead of them at length, side halls with more shops branching off along the way. More people ran toward Dane and Nina as they advanced. They reacted in fright when they saw Dane's gun. "We're here to help!" he said. "Run for the exit! Police on the way, go!" He shoved them in the right direction, he and Nina weaving through the short rush. Then they sprinted headlong toward the gunners.

The group of gunmen ran along the lower levels, blasting away. Dane braced on the rail. The .45 cracked in his hand, the gun spitting empty shells as fast as he pulled the trigger.

Two gunners out of the dozen fell, their blood smearing the tiled floor. Another gunner, shifting his position, slipped in a puddle and landed hard on his side. Nina shot him twice. A handful of gunners broke off and ran. Dane noticed one wore a heavy backpack.

He slapped a fresh mag into his gun.

"Gotta get down there," he said.

"Escalators back the way we came."

Dane and Nina reversed. Along the way they holstered their pistols and helped themselves to AKMs from the first set of dead shooters.

They reached the escalator in front of a Macy's and ran down, the AKMs leveled ahead of them. Some of the gunmen rushed their way. None of them wore a pack. Nina reached the floor first and broke right for a sitting area, firing as she moved. The gunmen scattered for cover. Dane's AKM hammered against his shoulder, the rounds tearing open a gunner's chest.

Dane advanced while Nina fired controlled bursts. Dane fired around the side of a kiosk. Gunmen scattered. More fell. Boots shuffled behind him. "Steve!" Dane whirled, swinging the butt stock of the AKM, slamming it into the face of a shooter sneaking up. As the shooter dropped, the muzzle of his weapon swung across Dane's belly. He tackled the gunner as the muzzle flashed, the flame searing his shoulder. The burst flew wide. Dane and the gunner landed hard, Dane rising to straddle the shooter and fire two rounds point blank into his chest.

Nina rushed over to him.

"Try and get any stragglers out of here," he said.

"Where are you going?"

"I have to find the guy with the backpack, it's another bomb."

"There's blood on your shirt!"

"It's not mine!"

Nina watched her man run to the last spot he'd seen the shooter with the backpack.

They'd been there too long already. Nina dropped the AKM and ran into the nearest shop.

"Anybody—"

A female cried out. Nina found three girls huddled in one corner, a male clerk under the counter. Nina gathered them to her and ushered them toward the nearest exit. She picked up a few strays along the way, trying to reassure them, but as they moved past dead and wounded along the way, she fell silent. There was no reassuring anybody in sight of the carnage.

The lack of gunfire meant the shooters were neutralized or had fled.

The JC Penny ahead was full of thick gray smoke. The target of the first two bombs. Dane ran to the Footlocker where he'd last seen the gunner with the backpack. Stopped short at a scrawl of red spray paint on a bare patch of wall.

Graypoole Has Resurrected.

No way.

No way!

The gunner ran out of the shoe store. No backpack anymore. Dane shot him in the face. Momentum carried the man forward some more but Dane was already running the other way. He dived and landed hard, sliding across the tiled floor to hut with a display of calendars, all torn up and tossed about. He scrambled behind cover and clamped both hands behind his neck. The explosion lifted him off the ground and slammed him down. He let out a yell, choking on smoke. He felt like he'd been punched in the gut. Gray smoke enveloped him.

His ears ringing, the only sound the pounding of the pulse in his head, Dane pushed to his feet and fought his way on rubbery legs through the smoke. His eyes burned, he couldn't breathe, but the graffiti flashed again through his mind.

Graypoole Has Resurrected.

Impossible!

As he staggered into a shop and collapsed on the carpet, somebody screamed. Dane looked up. His vision blurred but he saw human shapes in front of him. They needed help. He shuffled to hands and knees and reached out for them. As their hands clutched his and he led them out, another thought flashed through his mind.

What if Graypoole had?

Dane's vision started to clear as they neared the exit. The doors flung open and cops rushed in. Dane shouted there were still people hiding. Paramedics met him and his charges halfway out. A swarm of cop cars, fire engines and ambulances filled the street. Bystanders swarmed the area. Dane drifted away as the medics went to work.

He found Nina sitting against a wall. She rushed into his arms.

"We gotta scoot," she said.

"Too bad we didn't bring the rental," he said.

"TV's here."

"I'm more afraid of YouTube."

He leaned on her as they made their way through the chaos. Dane's legs started to return to normal. They made it across the street and leaned against the corner of a building. Dane, head down, tried to catch his breath. Nina rubbed his back.

"Steve," she said.

"Yeah?"

"Across the street, by the light pole. Bald man, no eyebrows."

Dane raised his head. His vision was still a little funky but he spotted the man in question. Watching the carnage. To anybody else, he was another passerby. But not to Dane and Nina.

"Hans Mueller," he said.

"Ready?"

"Let's take him."

CHAPTER 7

With Nina in the lead, they ran across the street. Mueller took off like a rabbit, pushing aside another couple. Dane and Nina dodged not only pedestrians but scattered debris, more light poles and shop sidewalk displays as Mueller knocked over anything in his path to block the way. Cracks in the sidewalk did not help Dane skidding around those obstacles to continue after his quarry. Mueller ran with his arms close to his body.

Behind him, Nina shouted she was crossing to the other side of the street.

Mueller leapt away from the curb, knocking over a man on a bicycle. Dane closed the gap. Mueller spun the bike around and started riding away, weaving around stopped cars. Dane slid across a hood, running between cars. Mueller pulled away, but not fast enough.

Dane grabbed the back of Mueller's coat, hauling him off the bicycle seat and slamming him onto the pavement. If anybody in the cars on the street were watching, Dane didn't see them. Mueller jumped up, throwing a lazy punch and Dane blocked, slamming a fist into the German's gut. Then Mueller wedged an elbow between them and smacked Dane in the jaw. Mueller shot his knee into Dane's midsection, Dane grunting as the pain of the impact filled his body.

Mueller ran, dodging bumpers, heading back toward the sidewalk. Nina yelled something as Dane clawed for his gun. He had to risk a shot. He lined up on Mueller's back as he turned into the garage of a hotel, but a coughing fit seized him, his lungs burning. He bent over and retched.

Dane straightened gasping as Nina ran up behind him.

"Come on, Steve."

"I can get him."

"Steve!"

"Let go of me, Nina!"

"He's gone! We have to get out of here!" she said.

Dane looked ahead. More people were watching, cops shouting for the observers to get out of the way. The men in uniform were approaching from down the street. Nina was right.

"Okay," he said.

She led him away.

Every television at CIA headquarters was tuned to a news station showing the live feed of the Westfield Shopping Center terror attack in San Francisco. Headline: Terror by the Bay.

In his office inside the Counter-Terror Division, Leonard Lukavina, sat behind his desk, eyes glued to the screen, not only upset about the attack but also the sensational headline at the bottom of the screen. He figured the network monkey who typed the words was probably very proud of himself.

Lukavina let out a breath and refocused. His mind raced to organize the answers to the inevitable questions soon to come his way. The first question would be, *"How did we miss this?"*

And the only answer Lukavina had at the moment was, *"I don't know."* The footage showed the exterior section of the mall, the black smoke still pouring from holes in the roof.

Lukavina glanced at the mug of now-cold coffee on his desk while playing absently with his wedding ring. Was it too soon to call home and say he'd be a week late for dinner?

Whoever carried out the attack had done so with exquisite planning and somehow managed to keep the communication between parties involved to a minimum. No informants had passed along any whisper of a strike, not even a thin rumor of the "I heard a guy who knows a guy who saw this guy who said he heard another guy say" variety. They'd had no warning.

At forty-six, Lukavina had been managing the CTD for three years and the unit had a high track record of preventing catastrophes, but this was a what-have-you-done-for-me-lately position. The brass on the seventh floor would only want to know how he missed this one.

He had been with the CIA for much longer than three years and had the marks to show for his experience. One side of his face appeared warped. The corner of one eye drooped and the lid didn't move when he blinked and he had to cover the bad eye with a patch at night. Lukavina had been one of the agents on Steve Dane's Blackhawk when it crashed and he was one of the last Dane pulled out of the wreckage before the chopper exploded. Lukavina took the most punishing blast of the explosion, nearly burning to death. So extensive had been the damage no amount of plastic surgery could fully erase the effects. The incident had forced his retirement from field work except on the rarest of occasions and on those occasions, he supervised from behind the scenes.

A glass wall with a centered door divided his raised office from the bull pen beyond, where analysts and his second-in-command worked. The door swung open. Debra Sloane, his number two and the woman in charge of CTD field operations, entered. She was in her late 50s with a fleshy face with red cheeks. Her suit was rumpled compared to the precision pressing of Lukavina's.

"Hear from the seventh floor?" she said.

Lukavina shook his head. "I'm dreading that call."

"We're already going through the recent updates. Len, there was *no* chatter about this."

"Sleeper cell? Lone wolf?"

"We are only guessing without hard data."

Lukavina cursed. Spinning wheels wasn't going to get them anywhere.

"Take a seat, Deb."

Debra found a chair near her boss's desk. They watched the television. Cops evacuated survivors. Paramedics tended the wounded. Firemen poured water from high-pressure hoses into the fire.

The shot changed to one of the Market Street entrance where the chaos and activity mirrored the other footage, but the wide angle showed periphery detail. The sight of one couple making their way from the scene made Lukavina sit up in his chair.

He grabbed the TV remote and froze the picture.

"Is that who I think it is?" Lukavina said.

A man leaned on a woman. His head was down but she

looked straight ahead. No mistaking her identity, even with the wide camera shot.

Debra examined the screen but only shrugged. "Who do you think it is, Len?"

"The woman is Nina Talikova. The man is Steve Dane. What are they doing there?"

"He's your friend. Why don't you—"

"I know, I know. I'll ask him."

He'd have something to tell the boss on the 7th floor after all, but he had tougher questions for Dane. If he'd been there during the attack, did he have prior knowledge? It wasn't like Dane to hold back from the authorities if he knew about a potential incident, but Dane wasn't perfect, either. Perhaps he and Nina had tried to prevent the attack at the last minute.

Either way, answers were forthcoming.

The DCI finally called and asked Lukavina to come up to his office.

Lukavina arrived within five minutes. He carried no files. Carlton Figg's secretary showed him in without saying hello.

Figg gestured to the chair in front of his desk. The desk sat in front of a wall displaying the CIA seal and an American flag. A wide window looking out on the crowded CIA parking lot and the green hills beyond took up one wall.

As he eased into the chairs, Lukavina noticed a stack of glossy photos on Figg's desk.

Figg was much older than Lukavina, a former army general, still in possession of his hair, though it was mostly gray. Figg had been DCI since the start of the new administration two years earlier.

"I don't want your head, Len, just tell me what we missed."

"I don't know. There's been no indication we faced an imminent attack."

"We're looking at two hundred casualties so far."

Figg handed Lukavina the pictures, but held one in reserve. Lukavina examined each photo. Police evidence shots. Shell casings marked. Bodies photographed. Some of the bodies had AKMs beside them.

"We had a mystery shooter taking out the bad guys."

"I think I know who, sir. Steve Dane."

"Why wouldn't he tell us if he had prior knowledge?"

"I haven't talked to him yet and I'd rather not speculate on an answer."

"Then we have this."

Figg handed over the last photo. It showed three words spray-painted on a wall.

Lukavina let out a curse. "Well today," he said, "keeps getting better."

"Graypoole is supposed to be dead," Figg said.

"Our people are *supposed* to discover attacks before they happen."

"Somebody else called the SFPD an hour after the bombing and said the same thing. 'Graypoole has resurrected.' Do we need a medium to find out what this means?"

"His son."

"Who?"

"Graypoole's kid."

"Taking over?"

"Best on-the-fly analysis I can offer, sir."

"Was he ever a suspect before?"

"Never. They were actually estranged. Junior stayed with his mother after she divorced the father."

"Why did she divorce him?"

"Didn't agree with his guerilla campaign. Graypoole released a manifesto announcing a war on capitalism. He started by murdering the top three CEOs listed in Fortune 500. Then he moved on to the club bombing in Geneva that killed fifty people, including four Marines. Our best intelligence at the time said the family wanted nothing to do with him, so they moved as far away as they could."

"Did we question the wife?"

"She gave us what she could. The son was a minor at the time. Graypoole still supported them, of course. Set up a trust-fund for the boy. Junior spent a lot of his father's money, typical playboy lifestyle. We watched him from time to time but he never showed any inclination to continuing his father's campaign." Lukavina offered a weak shrug. "I'm as surprised as you, sir."

Figg's eyes bored into Lukavina without blinking. He tapped a finger on the arm of his chair.

"Do we know where the mother is?"

"She passed away recently. Breast cancer."

Figg nodded. "I want an update in 24 hours, Len. Get back to work."

"Okay."

"And call Steve Dane."

"I have him on speed dial, sir."

CHAPTER 8

———◆———

Dane and Nina re-entered the hotel through a side entrance facing the Embarcadero, where they quickly stepped into an elevator for the fast ride to their suite. They looked like a bulldozer had rolled over them, but enough panic and concern over the events downtown filled the faces of those around them to allow their passage without notice.

Straight to the shower where they inspected the cuts and bruises and helped each other return to some state of normalcy. Dane's lungs hurt and he refused Nina's offer of a drink. She poured some vodka and joined him on the bed where they sat up and stared at the wall.

She finally turned on the television to have another sound in the room.

Footage and reports of the attack played on every local channel. The talking head chatter and faux-analysis almost lulled them to sleep. When a reporter introduced an interview with a witness, they perked up.

"There was a man and a woman running into the mall when we were trapped. They helped us get out and shot back at the attackers."

More talk and chatter about the identity of the couple, including whether or not they were with Homeland Security and did this mean the government knew about the attack but didn't tell anybody?

"Break out the tinfoil hats," Nina said.

Dane said nothing.

"Official sources," the reporter continued, *"will not confirm or deny the mystery couple was affiliated with U.S. law enforcement, but this hidden camera footage clearly shows the bodies of several dead attackers being carried out by a different exit and loaded into unmarked vans. Terry, back to you. . ."*

The blather went on and on.

"Can we find a reality show?" Nina said. "I need to replace some brain cells."

"We're going to get our own conspiracy page on Reddit after this," Dane said.

"I hate technology. I hate people, too."

"I'm wondering how long till the phone rings."

"I'm surprised it hasn't rung already," she said. "Your buddies in the CIA are probably too busy to care about us right now."

"Give 'em time."

She rubbed his leg. "Are you okay?"

"I keep seeing her face."

"Who?"

Dane told her.

"She wasn't the only one, Steve."

"She was the only one who looked straight at me. No matter what happens next, we're going to find out who did this and hand them their guts. No mercy."

Lukavina watched the bullpen from his office. Nobody was sitting still. They talked on the phone, typed furiously on computer keyboards, consulted each other over discoveries. Boxes of files sat on several desks, all of them marked with Graypoole's case number.

The television still showed footage from San Francisco, nothing new, but a constant loop of what had already been played several times already. As usual, the talking heads had everything wrong, although one or two who claimed "insider" status with the intelligence community tip-toed very close to the Graypoole story because the FBI hadn't been able to stop pictures of the graffiti in the mall from getting to the public.

Lukavina used a remote to turn off the set, then took out his cell phone. He pressed a button. After two rings, Steve Dane answered, but didn't say hello. He said:

"I had no idea, Len."

"What were you doing there?"

"On another job we finished the night before. We met the client at the mall to get his payment and were on our way out when the bomb went off."

"Tell me *everything* you saw, Steve."

Dane left out no detail. "I don't know what the bodies will tell you," he concluded, "but I can positively identify the bomber."

"How do you know?"

"Hans Mueller doesn't have eyebrows."

"He was there?"

"Watching the chaos like an arsonist who wants to see a building burn down. We tried to catch him but he got away."

"Gimme a second." Lukavina started typing on his computer. He logged onto the Agency's file database and punched in the German bomb maker's name. The screen flashed with Mueller's dossier, a picture of the man in the upper left corner.

"Mueller was last seen in Libya," Lukavina said. He scrolled through the file for more updates. "It was right after Graypoole was killed a year ago."

"Why wasn't Mueller whacked when you had the chance?"

"We didn't *get* the chance, Steve. He vanished. Graypoole's lieutenants all went underground. Dropped off the face of the earth. We'd figured Mueller contacted smugglers within the terror networks who helped him find a new place to hide."

"All right. How old is the dossier?"

"Steve—"

"If Graypoole's group is back together and active again, everything is now outdated. We need fresh stuff."

"What do you suggest?"

"We're going after Mueller. I'm calling my usual source as soon as I hang up. If he came out of hiding to plan this, he had to talk to people, who are talking to other people and we'll find him."

"That's *our* job, Steve."

"Then call it a freelance assignment at no cost to Uncle Sam."

"I don't have the authorization."

"*Get* it, Len. We aren't taking prisoners or leaving anything for the CIA to mop up. Get me? This kill is *mine*."

"I won't be around to bail you out if you get into trouble. If *Nina* gets you into trouble."

"You weren't in the gunfight, Len. You didn't see what I saw. This will be by-the-book. We aren't letting anybody get away this time."

Lukavina sighed. The attack must have been worse than he realized for Dane to behave in this manner. One could talk about how he wanted to protect the innocent and fight for those without a champion, but Dane did more than talk. Witnessing those he'd sworn to protect get cut down by terrorist bullets had galvanized him into action. The enemy had no chance.

"Don't get yourself killed in the process, buddy." It was the only thing the CIA could say. Once Dane was unleashed, there was no turning back.

"Bet on it. One more thing. What's the read on the graffiti? Is this going to be a zombie story or was Graypoole's death exaggerated?"

"We think it might be his kid."

"The deadbeat?"

"We won't know for sure until you crack Mueller."

"Send the info ASAP. We'll make Mueller talk."

"On the way."

Lukavina hung up and examined his computer screen some more. Between his people and the sources Dane cultivated, he should indeed have something to tell Figg before the 24-hour deadline. And he'd convince Figg to authorize Dane's freelance status for the mission. The man was putting his neck on the line; he deserved the backup. It wasn't the first time he was making a sacrifice for something bigger than him and it wouldn't be the last.

"Are you sure you're up for more?" Nina said.

"Last one," Dane said as he dialed a number. He sat on the edge of the bed, the hotel robe falling open a little, while she remained stretched out behind him, her glass empty on her lap.

The other line picked up.

"Yes?"

"It's me, Todd. Want some work?"

"Always," said Todd McConn.

Todd McConn had worked for Dane in the 30-30 Battalion and now cultivated and brokered information to interested parties. He still worked in the field now and then, especially when Dane called, but spent most of his time at what he called the Mississippi Strongbase.

McConn was Dane's main source of intelligence regarding covert matters.

He had another source for weapons and equipment.

"Hear about San Francisco?" Dane said.

"Yeah."

"What do you know about Graypoole?"

"Every snitch is scrambling on this one. Nobody saw it coming."

"I have a lead I need you to get started on," Dane said. "Nina and me are coming to you first thing tomorrow."

"Okay, shoot."

"I need everything you have on Hans Mueller."

"The bomber?"

"Yup." Dane explained his encounter with the German on the streets of San Francisco and his chat with Lukavina officially bringing him into the case. "We need to find him and make him talk. Whether or not he remains in one piece when we finish remains to be seen."

"I'll have a full workup by the time you get here. Bring me what CIA sends you so we can laugh about how wrong they are."

"I'm in no mood for jokes this time, Todd."

Jose Ramos stopped the car outside a small cafe.

It was his first visit to Valencia's Marina Real Juan Carlos, where the rich tourists parked their toys. A long jetty extended into the ocean, the slips alongside filled with yachts of various sizes and colors, from plain white to blue and gold. A pair of trim deckhands wearing white shirts and trousers cleaned the windows on one, while a pair of sunbathers lay out on the rear deck of another. An older woman in a black one piece lounged on a chair near the rail of yet another yacht, sipping a glass of wine.

Seagulls fluttered about the parking lot near the café, which was before the jetty.

Ramos took a deep breath. His pulse beat rapidly. He hadn't been this exposed in over a year, since the assassination of his boss, but Graypoole the Younger had made a personal request to see him and Ramos couldn't turn away. He and his wife, who operated as a pair, had been in hiding long enough. When news of the strike in San Francisco, with the associated signature, finally reached them, they hoped they'd be reactivated next.

Sometimes dream do come true.

He pulled a pair of binoculars from the glove box and carefully exited the car, looking around. No sign of anybody watching, and those hovering around were focused on their own leisure—loafing was hard work.

Ramos was confident the call hadn't been part of a set-up. But he took nothing for granted. After San Francisco, US intelligence would be combing the world for Mueller, Ramos and anybody else formerly associated with Graypoole.

He stayed near the cafe building, following the back wall to the corner. The breeze carried the scent of salt and seaweed. The seagulls squawked behind him. Through the binoculars he looked at a yacht at the very end, the largest of all, gold in color, the sleek front end tapering almost into an arrow point. The railed sundeck had a table-and-chairs set, while the open-air bridge showed the latest in radar antenna. The tinted windows below decks hid what lay behind.

Ramos zeroed in on the yacht's name. *Espinosa II.*

Graypoole Senior's old yacht. No mistake.

Ramos put the binoculars back in the car and entered the cafe. No bell above the door. Tables lined the panoramic windows which offered a view of the ocean. Only a few people sat at the tables, either couples or small groups, sipping coffee or wine and dressed in designer clothes.

Ramos was well-dressed but not as young as the other patrons. French intelligence had nicknamed him "Carlos Jr." for his resemblance to a young Carlos the Jackal. He hailed from Venezuela and had a chubby face and barrel chest like his faux-namesake. Unlike his namesake, nobody had captured—or killed—him yet.

A woman sitting a few spaces down the counter had blonde hair and a big nose and wore a pink silk scarf around her neck. A disguise. His wife insisted on them. He sat down beside her.

"Anything?"

"All clear," said Kassandra Ramos.

He gave her the name of the yacht and told her to come in shooting if he didn't return in twenty minutes.

CHAPTER 9

■———■

Ramos entered the salon and froze at the sight of the man before him.

The big yacht felt still below his feet. The deckhand went to a mini bar on the side and started pouring drinks. The salon was opulently appointed with lots of dark wood, leather, soft carpet, and gold trim. The port windows were open, letting in the afternoon breeze and the scent of salt and fish.

Ramos opened his mouth to say something, but suddenly words failed him. His mind filled with flashbacks of the elder Graypoole singing the praises of his son and the rest of the crew instead seeing a wanna-be playboy who would never live up to his father's hype. The young man before him, however, was not the same Mason Graypoole he'd known before. *This* Mason Graypoole looked fitter. He looked like he could handle himself in a fight. He looked like he'd put the past behind him and finally realized his potential.

And what a tragedy he could not fight by his father's side.

"Hello, Jose," Mason Graypoole said. "Thank you for coming."

Graypoole sat at a large table, the edges gold-lined.

The tan leather booth matched the color of the table. The deckhand set a glass in front of Graypoole and handed one to Ramos on his way out. The galley door clicked shut.

Ramos remained standing.

"You're looking good. Lose a little weight?"

Ramos offered a weak smile in response.

"Were you followed?"

Finally Ramos said, "No."

"I know you took a big risk coming here."

"My wife and I have been running. And hiding. A lot. I know about Mueller and San Francisco. We'd like a chance to get even. Are you offering such a chance?"

"Yes."

Mason Graypoole's blue eyes were alive with the fire of enthusiasm Ramos had also seen in his father's. The apple didn't fall far from the tree at all, though it had taken time. Graypoole's straight black hair touched the base of his neck and his blue suit hadn't come off the rack. Savile Row and no mistake. Like his father.

Ramos joined him at the table and raised the glass to his lips. He swallowed the bourbon. Knob Creek. At least it wasn't cheap.

Graypoole lifted a tablet computer from the cushion beside him and switched it on. "I've been planning this for over a year." He showed Ramos the document on the screen. "First, San Francisco. Mission accomplished. Next, we target General Walker when he takes a trip to Rome."

"Isn't he—"

"No longer part of special operations. Walker was injured in a car accident. Now he rides a desk at the Pentagon to finish out his last few years before retirement."

"Uh-huh."

"Then there's the matter of Mr. Kader, who thinks he's

safe in Bahrain. I'll shoot him myself."

"Uh-huh."

Graypoole swiped left and showed Ramos the next document. "The last part of my plan is my favorite and involves you and Kassandra. There's nobody else I want on the job."

Ramos took the tablet and read the document. He let out a whistle.

"Is that a yes?"

Ramos handed back the tablet and watched Graypoole's eyes. His gaze didn't waver.

Ramos said, "What do you want?"

"What do you mean?"

"I need to know why we're doing this."

"We're picking up where my father left off."

"Starting with revenge?"

"Yes, Jose. What *else* do we start with? I don't know if I hate capitalism as much as my father, or if I agree global communism is a worthy goal, but I do know I want to get even. I want to kill the people responsible for killing my father. We start with General Walker. Then Mr. Kader, who sold out my father to the Americans. We knock them down like dominos, Jose."

"But what you want Kassandra and me to do—"

"Just like Mueller, your job is more in line with something my father would ask of you, isn't it?"

"It is."

"Then what is your answer, Jose?"

"We'll do it."

"Good!" Graypoole's smiled flashed again. "Can you leave immediately?"

"We'll be on the next plane," Ramos said. "Not under our own names, of course."

"I'll forward the information on the tablet to your email or wherever else you want it," Graypoole said. "Good luck."

Ramos felt a warm glow inside.

Gloomy gray clouds greeted Jose and Kassandra Ramos as they stepped off the Delta 737 at Seattle/Tacoma International Airport.

They did not travel under their real names and also did not resemble the photos in the dossiers of the world's intelligence and law enforcement agencies. Their departure had not been hasty. As two people on the run, always prepared to flee from one place to another, find another safe haven under extreme adversity, they always had bags packed and lived only with the bare necessities. In other words, they traveled light.

Kassandra Ramos did not skimp on her disguise. She kept her usual wig-and-scarf combo, a brunette this time, the pink scarf wrapped a little tighter with the Seattle chill biting through her leather jacket.

Ramos couldn't remove any of his bulk but he could alter his face a little, with a goatee and mustache, each touched with a little gray, with the bottom of his right shoe filed off to give him a slight limp. The little things counted.

They left the airport property in a rental and followed Highway 5 south. Graypoole had secured a safe house for them to operate from. Kassandra plugged the address into the car's in-dash GPS and a voice with a British accent directed them along the route.

Kassandra glanced at her husband, who kept his eyes focused ahead, scanning traffic. He wouldn't talk during the drive. Because he was driving. He needed total concentration. It made her laugh. She didn't understand why he performed the task with such intensity.

She'd grown up with her father, a lawyer and Marx-ist, enthralling her from a young age with stories of the revolution in Cuba and elsewhere in the world where the people lived with equality and fairness; with shared re-sponsibilities, material items, and property. Her writings for left-wing publications at Paris Sorbonne brought her to the attention of one of the many factions on campus recruiting students.

She met Jose Ramos at a secret meeting where Ramos gave the keynote about how they were the only ones who could bring about the kind of social change the world needed. The group offered more than simply *talk*, which Kassandra was tired of, but action against the one percent and the other ills of society kept the People from assuming their proper place.

It was during Ramos's speech where Kassandra fell in love with him. He had the usual Latin good looks and his suit fit him amazingly well.

She made her commitment and stayed close to Ramos where he finally noticed her. He taught her to shoot and build bombs and she let him seduce her.

They were inseparable except when duty forced them apart. They tried not to let interruptions happen very often.

She turned up the heater as Ramos sped along under the highway limit. The dashboard temperature gauge said it was 58 degrees outside, made chillier by the mist hanging in the air.

"We should go see the Space Needle if we have time," she said.

Ramos only grunted.

"Bill Gates' also lives here, you know."

Ramos made another sound. "Biggest enemy of them

all."

"Should we save some C-4?"

Ramos's eyes never stopped scanning the road. "Maybe next time."

Presently Ramos turned off the freeway and they followed city streets to the suburbs, where the narrow streets dipped on either side to help keep standing water from accumulating on the pavement. Yards were full of lush green lawns and the multiple colors of a wide variety of flowers kept Kassandra's attention as they moved.

Ramos finally slowed and turned into a driveway cluttered with leaves, a raised crack a few feet from the sidewalk. Ramos let the front wheels go over the crack and stopped the car. He and Kassandra regarded the small house before them curiously.

"This is better than a hotel?" Ramos said.

The house had puke-green paint with a large porch and brick smoke stack on one side. Messy yard. The grass was overgrown, half-dead bushes and trees covering most of the porch.

"I'm sure it's nice inside," Kassandra said. They left the car and carried their bags into the house. "See?" she said. "Much better."

The interior was the exact opposite. Wood floors, white walls, every room furnished with antique-looking items Kassandra said provided a certain charm to the place. Ramos went to the kitchen and tested the faucet in the sink. Cold water ran strong. He investigated the hallway bathroom as well, turning on the shower a moment. He came out of the hall wiping a wet hand on his pants.

"It will do," he said. "At least we're not paying for it."

They found the master bedroom at the very end of the hall and loaded the dresser with their clothes.

"We should hit the store for supplies," Ramos said.

"I'll make a list."

She investigated cupboard and refrigerator space in the kitchen, finding more than enough room. Usual counter, kitchen table, with a separate breakfast nook near a window looking out on a back yard as equally overgrown as the front. More wood and white. No attention to other colors or decorative arrangements.

"A man owns this," Kassandra said to herself.

A blast of air rumbled through the vents. "Heater works," Ramos announced.

It was as good a safe house as they could want, Kassandra decided. The front yard partially concealed the living room windows. Plenty of cover for their activities. And because it was ugly in front, nobody would pay much attention to what went on within.

Kassandra removed her wig and scarf. She had close-cropped black hair and a very small nose, which matched her small mouth and lips. She made a grocery list and started for the front door. Stepping onto the porch, something skittered off to her left. She saw the back end of a cat slither under the porch rail to hide in the bushes. The cat peered back at her through the leaves.

"Hi," she said. She squatted down. The cat, tense, stared at her. "Do you live here too?" The cat's eyes stayed fixed on her. The animal looked very bony and thin with no body mass. She looked over the warped wood of the porch, the peeled paint, cracks. She could put out a bowl of food. The cat slithered under the porch, its long tail the last to slide beneath the wood. Kassandra stood and went to the car. Driving away, she wondered if she should tell Jose about the cat. He didn't like cats.

It was his only flaw.

CHAPTER 10

The girl and her father were buried together.

Her name had been Lilly Klove, her father James Klove and Dane and Nina watched their funeral from a distance. The mourners, all in black, had left the funeral service a few minutes earlier and now stood at the graveside as the caskets were lowered and final words spoken.

Nina watched Dane. His eyes were fixed, unblinking, on the gathering. Lilly and her father were being laid to rest at Cypress Lawn Memorial Park in Colma, a city where the dead outnumbered the living, the population of the departed growing as more victims of the San Francisco Bombing, as it was becoming known, were interred. San Francisco no longer allowed burials in city limits after a 1900 city ordinance. Anybody unlucky to pass in the City by the Bay was shipped south to Colma or wherever a family decided to lay their dead.

Standing amongst the gray headstones, green grass, blue sky and otherwise peaceful area, Nina knew, did nothing to calm the blood boiling in Dane's veins. There had been more than one innocent victim in the mall bombing, but the girl represented them all. She'd fallen in Dane's arms. Nina also knew he probably blamed himself for not forcing her out of there faster.

Or not jumping in front of the bullets.

She rubbed his back. He brushed her arm away. His gaze remained fixed on the gravesite.

On their previous visit to San Francisco, where Dane had lost a friend after responding to his call for help, he had revealed to Nina something he admitted never telling anybody else. As a young man, he'd tried to keep his distance from death, whether it was his grandparents or pets, because he didn't want to deal with the emotions. It wasn't until later in life where he finally let himself grieve for previous losses and felt like life was dealing him a bad hand with all the fatalities he'd since been surrounded with. Friends and enemies alike. There was no hiding from death now. He had to face it at every turn, like he was facing it now.

Nina turned her attention to the burial. The caskets were in the ground, the group breaking apart slowly, wandering back to vehicles. It was over so fast. Nina was always struck by how quickly such moments began and ended but always lingered in the mind.

Dane finally let out a breath.

She looked at him. His face had softened. Maybe now he'd say something.

"What now?" Nina said.

He turned his head and locked eyes with her.

"No more victims," he said. "Let's go."

He turned sharply and started walking. Nina hurried to catch up. She knew there would be more victims, but she and Steve would give their all to keep the numbers as low as possible.

Meanwhile, they had a plane to catch.

Time to even the score.

Their flight left SFO on time. Nina leaned back in her seat to sleep but Dane stayed awake and stared out the window.

He didn't have any deep thoughts about the mission. Find Mueller, make him talk. Dane had been active too long to give the enemy any further thought than one gave a cockroach on the kitchen floor.

But he kept seeing the girl's face. Her big brown eyes stayed on him. She wouldn't rest until her killers were dealt with. Dane didn't blame her.

He'd read the CIA's file on Mueller prior to the funeral, but still wasn't sure if they could use any of the details. Once he saw McConn's intelligence and found matching points in both files, he'd have a better idea about what to plan.

Nina snorted but didn't wake up. Dane asked for a Coke when the flight attendants passed with the service cart and one handed him a bag of mixed nuts as well. No first class amenities or first class at all on such a short flight.

Nina awoke before the plane touched down in Memphis and McConn met them at baggage claim.

Todd McConn looked like a cross between a California surfer and a cowboy. Wiry frame on which his clothes hung loosely, long hair, T-shirt and jeans, with cowboy boots and Stetson rounding out the ensemble.

Smiles and handshakes with a hug for Nina as the three greeted each other and McConn led the way to his dirty Subaru wagon. It didn't look like much, but the engine was strong and McConn had replaced the soft factory suspension with a racing set-up. The wagon cornered like it was on rails.

Nina called shotgun so Dane hopped in the back seat after loading their suitcases.

"From one job to another, huh?" McConn said as he drove. Not from the South, he had no accent. He'd chosen Memphis as a home base because of a smoking property deal he found.

"You find out anything about Mueller?" Dane said.

"Some good stuff, yeah. You're gonna like it."

Presently McConn turned up an unpaved driveway and followed a long access road. Trees lined either side with green grass covering the rest of the property. A three-story colonial sat dead center, with a circular driveway and wrap-around porch.

"I kept the outside original," McConn said, "but inside is all remodeled. Hard-wood flooring, modern electrical system, central heating and air conditioning. Spared no expense."

"No wainscoting?" Dane said.

"Good heavens, no."

They left their bags in the front room. Off to the left and right of the entryway sat the dining room and living room, each well-appointed, with a set of steps ahead which McConn said led to his basement operations center. He promised a full tour later and led them down the steps.

The basement had plenty of space, some of it occupied by computer and monitoring equipment and the rest looked like storage of a variety of items. Dane noted a gun case in one corner. One wall was dedicated to a computer and several monitors, with a large flat screen monitor on the next wall.

"Welcome to my office," McConn said as he strapped on a pistol belt. The 9mm Beretta 92FS on his hip tipped

forward in the holster.

"What's that for?" Dane said.

"I have a client mad at me."

"Really?"

"I sold him some information he didn't act on for a week. By the time he did, the information was outdated. He accused me of selling him faulty intelligence, some threats have been exchanged and I'm taking precautions."

"Oh, brother," Nina said.

"You could have told me ahead of time."

"It's not a big deal, Steve. There are sensors all over the property and plenty of combat space," McConn said. A cluster of security monitors to the left of McConn showed different parts of the property. "If even a bird lands on the grass, I'll know about it."

He pulled out a chair and sat down in front of computer. "I'll put everything on the big screen," he said.

Dane stood by Nina and waited. He raised an eyebrow at her. She shook her head.

McConn dimmed the lights and started typing. The screen filled with Hans Mueller's bald dome.

"We know what he looks like, ding-dong."

"Want to see where he lives?"

"Currently? Like right now?"

"Like right now, yeah. CIA doesn't have that, do they?"

"No."

A few more keystrokes showed an angled, above-ground shot of a cabin in the woods, an A-frame with smoke drifting from the chimney.

"Just outside Berlin. Current location. Sat scan confirms."

"How can you tell?"

"Top of his head, for one. Plus, he likes to step out and

look at the weather."

Dane stepped closer to the screen. The glow lit up his face. "Any other angles?"

Two other pictures flashed, side angles and a long shot of the front. "Couldn't get much closer," McConn said.

"You're positive he's there?"

A fourth picture showed Mueller on the porch along with two other men, both lingering around the driveway in front of the cabin. The top of Mueller's head didn't mean much to Dane, but McConn switched to another shot of Mueller looking up at the sky. Good enough for Dane.

"How long's he been there?"

"Not long. Couple weeks. My contacts say he always has at least two guards at the place. They're mercenaries. Two stay at the cabin while two others live in the loft above a bar in Berlin owned by one of Mueller's buddies. They rotate weekly."

"Who brings the replacements?"

"Mueller's girlfriend, Lanka."

Another picture flashed on-screen. A woman with dark skin, dark hair, big brown eyes. She wore a long red dress and carried a diamond-studded purse.

"Lanka Kobevko," McConn said. "Ukrainian. She's been going with Mueller for a couple of years."

"What's her background?" Nina said.

"Party girl. She hung around the periphery of anarchist groups until she met Mueller at a rally."

"How did she hook up with Mueller?" Nina said.

"Not sure."

"She visits once a week to bring the replacement guards," Dane said, "and she lives in Berlin?"

"Uh-huh."

Dane cursed under his breath. The CIA wasn't a bad

organization. Good people worked there who wanted to do their best and protect the US, but for all the good they did, when they dropped the ball on something, they dropped it hard. Lukavina had told Dane, Mueller had vanished after fleeing to Libya. Fine. But to lose track of him entirely, fall into the trap of "out of sight out of mind" was inexcusable and part of the reason the San Francisco bombing had taken place.

But there was no sense in complaining. They had the lead they needed and the ability to strike back.

"Let's start there," Dane said. "Want to come along?"

"I could use a break from the house, yeah," McConn said.

"Good," Dane said. "We'll call Devlin as well. We leave first thing tomorrow."

A buzzer sounded and a red light flashed on one of the security screens.

McConn rolled his chair to the monitor. Dane joined him.

"Three guys hopping the eastern fence," McConn said. The monitor plainly showed the three men and they all toted automatic weapons.

"Your angry clients?"

"Looks like."

"Our guns are packed."

McConn jerked a thumb over his shoulder. "Cabinet."

Nina went to the indicated corner and opened both cabinet doors. A variety of semi-automatic rifles and pistols were inside. She grabbed two handguns and passed one to Dane. Dane exchanged the handgun for a Mossberg 500 12-gauge shotgun and a handful of shells. He started feeding the rounds into the tube.

"We have to wait for them to come into the house," McConn said.

"Why?" Dane stuffed spare shells into his pockets.

"Because then it's legal to kill them."

"No prisoners," Nina said, snapping a shell into her automatic.

"Exactly." McConn took out his Beretta. "Follow me." He started for the stairs.

out into the back yard, but Dane saw no sign of hostiles.

McConn stayed low as he entered the living room, using the furniture for cover. None of the windows seemed disturbed and he found nobody hiding anywhere. He moved across to a doorway, entering a short hallway. To the right, the door to the side porch; kitchen on the left. He stepped into the kitchen. He and Dane turned their guns on one another but quickly removed fingers from triggers.

"On the deck!" McConn said.

He and Dane dropped behind the center island as a gunman blasted the patio door, slipping into the house. McConn rose first, the two shots from his Beretta snapping loudly. The gunman twisted out of the way, the shots going wide, but then Dane, firing from the floor, blasted out the man's left knee. The shooter screamed. McConn followed up with a headshot and the shooter stopped screaming.

Nina cut through the dining area to the larger adjoining room McConn had set up with a pair of pool tables, bar, and a sitting area of leather couches, all of it brightly lit from the windows and ceiling skylight. Her shoes landed hard on the wood floor. The home she and Dane shared wasn't this nice. You could eat off the floor. The goon entering through the shot-out window behind the bar saw her and fired, ducking under the bar as Nina rolled under a pool table.

She'd selected a Browning Hi-Power, a nine-millimeter pistol with a 13-round magazine, the magazine loaded with hard-nosed slugs. More than able to penetrate the wood of the bar. She fired a line of shots into the front, the wood splitting, but nobody screamed. She fired another pair of rounds into another section.

The gunman rose and fired back, the top of the pool table splitting open, wood shards flying everywhere. Nina

CHAPTER 11

$—\blacksquare—$

Automatic gunfire punched through the front door.

"Down!" Dane shouted, throwing himself at Nina. The trio landed hard on the stairs, wood splinters flying everywhere and sizzling projectiles slamming into the interior of the house. The door flew open as the man on the other side gave it a kick. Dane jumped up with the shotgun pressed into his shoulder. He squeezed the trigger. The blast of buckshot ripped open the gunman's chest and stomach, bloody guts and pieces of bone joining the mess on the entryway. The gunman's body landed with a squishy thud.

Dane pumped another round and waited.

Glass broke somewhere; another shot cracked.

"They've spread out," McConn said, running up the rest of the stairs. Dane and Nina took off in separate directions.

Dane, behind McConn, made a left as McConn entered the living room. Dane advanced down the foyer hallway, kitchen ahead, the shotgun at the ready. He stopped at the corner. The kitchen counter was spotless; the center island also clean; the tiles nicely polished. Did McConn do housework all day? A window above the sink looked slithered around on the wood floor and crawled on knees and elbows for the other pool table behind her.

She rolled under the table, fired twice without aiming, the gunman ducking back. Then the gunman rolled out from behind and returned fire, his automatic weapon spitting flame. The table leg closest to Nina splintered, the leg falling on her head. She shook it free and scooted back as the gunman blasted the leg off to her left. The pool table toppled and crashed onto the floor. Nina leaped up and ran around the side, bringing her pistol up as the gunman also rose with his own weapon aimed at her. She started to pull the Browning's trigger when a shotgun blast opened the side of the gunman's head like a popped balloon. Gory skull fragments splattered and flaps of flesh dangled on the side of the man's head. The gunman dropped. Nina lowered her gun. Dane and McConn stepped into the room.

"I had him," she said.

Dane pumped the shotgun. "I'll wait longer next time." He winked.

They spent the rest of the day and well into evening talking with the cops who filled the house. Squad cars and other official vehicles littered the front of the property. The trio stuck to the same story. They were catching up and suddenly the three gunmen decided to invade the home. No idea who they were, what they wanted, etc., etc., and some of the cops speculated it was drug related. McConn didn't correct them. Memphis had a horrible drug and gang problem, so it wasn't unrealistic. McConn told the cops the goons had picked the wrong house.

They, of course, couldn't stay at the house so the cops let McConn pack a few things. Dane and Nina were already packed. While the house, now a crime scene, was sealed, Dane, Nina, and McConn checked into a hotel downtown. McConn was under orders not to leave town, but he had a way around the order thanks to his lawyer, who could act as his representative while he left on a pre-scheduled business trip, i.e.: the mission with Dane. He'd need the money from the job to pay for fixing the house and pay his lawyer for fixing the cops.

At the hotel, they ate a light dinner in the lobby restaurant.

"Sorry we made a mess of your place," Dane said.

McConn waved it off. "I'll rebuild."

"What do you do all day?" Nina said. "Your house was way too clean. Do you walk around with a mop and Pinesol?"

"Do you have a problem with being orderly?"

Nina scoffed and polished off three vodka tonics during the meal while McConn and Dane left their beers unfinished. After dinner they went up to their rooms. The rooms weren't adjoining; McConn was on the floor above Dane and Nina.

"We start early tomorrow," Dane told McConn as the three said good-night.

His leg hurt a little more as he rolled out of bed.

General Curtis Walker groaned and rubbed his left leg through pajama pants. Typical morning. His left foot was numb, but his exercises would eventually wake it up. Worst case, he had a cane leaning against the nightstand. He liked to remember he'd shot the bastard who had tossed the grenade resulting in his injury, but the thought never gave Walker any solace. The doctors had put him back together, but pieces of shrapnel remained under his skin.

One of the side-effects was a temporarily numb foot, every single morning. And the chance of infection from the shrapnel. A visit to the doctor every other month helped keep an eye on that. So far, so good. He had to keep telling people the injury was the result of a car accident and not a secret mission, but little lies no longer bothered him.

He rolled over and sat up. His wife, Penny, already started the day and he could smell coffee and bacon. He dropped to the floor, rolled onto his back and began lifting his legs and engaging in flutter kicks, locking his knees and moving his legs up and down in a scissor motion. He kept his arms stretched out beside him. Starting slowly, he eventually built some speed and worked up a bit of a sweat. He stood up, testing his left leg and when he could put his weight on his left foot comfortably, he made his way to the bathroom.

After a shower he put on his Class A uniform and went downstairs. He used to hate those stairs. All the up and down, up and down. . . but they actually helped his leg, and now he appreciated them.

Walker entered the kitchen, where Penny was putting breakfast on their plates.

"Good morning, sweetheart," he said and kissed her.

"Leg okay?"

He took his place at the table. "Nothing more than usual."

The morning paper sat on the table. Walker looked at the front page. The latest on the bombing in San Francisco. He set the paper aside. He would have enough about the bombing and Graypoole to read about at work. He didn't actively participate in special ops any longer, but his tasks at the Pentagon still involved secret work. He was in charge of the Pentagon's office of army intelligence. He rode a desk and kept up-to-date on operations carried out by others and it made him feel useless. The office job gave him not only his one-star status but the opportunity to retire with thirty-five years, and he wanted his full pension more than action. But the routine wore him down. He often wondered if he should have taken retirement early, but it was too late to make a change. He had to fulfill the commitment.

Penny came over to the table with Walker's eggs and bacon and a bowl of fruit and set them down in front of him. He said thank you and started eating.

They had designed the kitchen themselves when purchasing the house. Penny had wanted everything big. Lots of room for company and family. Walker's contribution had been a small nook for a table and bench seats in a corner. An intimate place for meals when it was only them, which it had been, off and on, when their daughters were in college. Now the girls were well beyond college, so it had been only them for the last few years. It had been hard to adjust and both were looking forward to a long vacation with the girls.

"There are only a few days left until we leave for Rome," Penny said with a smile. She sipped her coffee. Most of her black hair was gray now, but some of the original color held on for dear life. Her nose always crinkled when she smiled, but now there were a few extra wrinkles mixed it.

They'd been married almost forty years, but mornings hadn't always been this peaceful. When the kids were growing up, mornings were quite chaotic. Both girls were on their own, neither married yet, but both had growing careers.

"The girls seem really excited," Walker said as he ate a piece of bacon.

"So am I. Are you?"

The general wasn't known for his effervescent personality.

"Yes," he said. "Won't hurt to get away from the office after the last few days."

"You're not going to read the paper?"

He shook his head. "I've had enough bad news."

After breakfast he helped with the dishes and kissed Penny goodbye. Walker drove with a cup of coffee in his hand and the radio tuned to the local sports station where he listened to the chatter about the previous night's Redskins game. He approached the check-point to the Pentagon's south parking lot and stopped. The guard on-duty checked his ID. Always the same guard, always the same routine. "Good morning, General. Go on through."

"Thank you, Sergeant." Walker headed into the lot and eased the Lincoln into his assigned spot. He downed the rest of his coffee and set his mug on the passenger seat. The battered brown leather briefcase he had used since his command of the First Special Forces Battalion sat in the back seat. The case had seen more action and more secrets than he had, it seemed. He reached back and grabbed it.

The sprawling five-sided building with the Potomac on the other side towered high above him as he walked through the front glass doors. It wasn't an impressive or even imposing sight. It looked like a regular office building.

"Morning, General," the guard at the front desk said. The sign-in book was open to a blank page. A pen lay next to it. Walker signed his name and stepped into the elevator behind the desk.

The General entered his office five minutes later and his assistant, Sergeant First Class Julie Fisher, held up some mail. "These came in for you, sir."

"What are they?" He took the offered envelopes.

"Evaluation reports, I believe. I put some memos on your desk, too. Also, General Taylor made an appointment to see you later this afternoon around three-thirty. He said it concerns the upcoming joint exercise between us and Britain next month."

Walker nodded. "Thank you, Sergeant." He entered his office and sat down behind his desk. The window behind him looked out over the river. It was a nice perk. He set the mail on his desk and glanced at the calendar near a lamp. Only a few more days. A few more very long days.

CHAPTER 12

Kassandra Ramos parted the curtains and looked at the porch.

The kitty cat, with its rear end high, ate eagerly from the bowl of dry food she had put out, crunching and swallowing probably a little too fast, but Kassandra wasn't about to go out and disturb the animal.

"Kassandra."

She turned. Ramos stood near the hallway, jacket on, briefcase in hand.

"Forget the cat. We need to get going before we spend all day in traffic."

"Oh, honey," she said. "You can turn it off once in a while, you know."

She brushed past him and went down the hall.

Ramos drove, his concentration once again one-hundred percent on the road. Kassandra reviewed some notes she had made the night before.

The wet mist still hung in the air and the clouds remained with the ominous threat of a sudden downpour, but as they turned off Highway 5 and proceeded to the corner of Pike and 7th Ave., none of the rain emerged.

Traffic wasn't bad and Ramos stopped briefly for the light at Pike and 7th before making a right turn, then another left. A second left brought them to the garage entrance of the Washington State Convention Center. The steel-and-glass structure, with concrete support columns at each corner, occupied the whole block, the windows reflecting the gloomy skies, almost multiplying the dreariness. Across the street were the Hyatt and Roosevelt Hotels.

Ramos took a parking ticket from the automatic machine, the blocking bar lifted, and they found a spot in the sparsely populated garage. Both exited without a word and quickly made their way back to the street, the polished cement floor clean of tire streaks or oil spots. They followed the sidewalk around the corner to the front of the convention center.

They stood to one side as other pedestrians went by. Nobody gave them a second look. Traffic moved briskly. Kassandra consulted her notes.

"It's all here," she said.

Ramos studied the scenery. "Shops and restaurants all around, plenty of people. This is a good spot."

"Can we go inside?"

"I'm sure it's open."

They went up the steps of the convention center and Ramos held the door open for his wife. The glass door shut behind them and blocked out most of the outside noise. A heater's hum filled the interior, which was toasty warm compared with the outside chill. Their shoes tapped on the tiled floor as they wandered through the lobby. The walls were made of tiered levels of glass. Beyond the glass, an outdoor area full of green hedgerows and trees. They crossed to a display beside an empty reception desk and read the list of the upcoming events:

International Conference on Robotics & Automation
May 24th - May 31st
Law Seminars Int'l: Hydrology and the Law
May 29th
Symposium on Cyber Security
June 6th

"D-Day," Kassandra said.

Ramos smiled. "I'm sure Graypoole enjoys the irony."

The symposium wasn't simply on cyber security, but an opportunity for the top CEOs and leaders in the industry to display their latest and greatest products.

In other words, the perfect target. Ramos would like nothing better than to see a bunch of tech leaders dead in the street. They all seemed to believe they were gods, yielding power at will, when they were only a step or two above the average mindless rat who depended on them for sustenance. Tech CEOs, with their inflated egos, loved the attention, loved being treated like a god, thriving in the spotlight as their minions knelt before their brilliance. Like all religions, it was fake. The only religion worthy of the name, of devotion, was the People. Tech leaders had no interest in people. They were interested only in erasing people and replacing them with machines. They wanted to enslave the people by forcing them to spend money on their widgets and doo-dads, creating a dependence upon machines and gadgets, which added nothing to their quality of life and, in fact, stole from it.

Ramos would take great delight in destroying them all, watching as their smug expressions vanished in a flash of violence. He and Kassandra continued their self-guided tour but didn't see any convention center staff. A set of open doors led to one of the concourse areas where a group of people in street clothes were setting up tables and displays for the robotics conference.

Back outside, Kassandra shivered. She zipped up her coat.

"No office or security staff," Ramos said.

"Upper levels?" she said.

Ramos looked back at the building. Four stories total. "Probably."

Kassandra pointed across the street. "Won't matter."

"Hmmm?"

"See that airport shuttle?"

The yellow-and-blue van, with the hotel logo on the side and "Airport Shuttle" below, pulled up in front of the Hyatt's entrance.

"It would fit, don't you think?"

"Sure," Ramos said. "Nobody will look twice."

Crossing the street, they boarded the shuttle. The driver told them they'd be departing in a few minutes as he stepped off. They settled into a seat in the middle of the bus.

The ride to SeaTac was uneventful and it solved exactly how to get one of those shuttle buses on June 6th.

D-Day, indeed.

General Walker returned from lunch to find an FBI agent waiting in the outer office. Sergeant Fisher stopped him and introduced the agent.

"Can we talk in your office?" the agent said. His name was Burke and he wore a perfectly pressed gray suit, hair combed straight back, with well-manicured nails. Everything a G-Man should be.

Walker frowned at him. "Can't take too long."

"Five minutes at the most."

Walker led Burke inside. The G-man remained standing while he sat. "What's up, Agent Burke?"

"You're aware of what happened in San Francisco?" the agent said.

"Yes."

"There is some concern you'll be the next target."

"Who sent you?"

"I'm following-up for friends at the CIA."

"Are you making a joke?"

Burke smiled. "Seriously, General, have you noticed anybody following you? Your family?"

"Not at all, Agent Burke."

"I'm not authorized to offer protection, but you can go through channels to request it."

"I'll talk to my guys here. CID can cover me if it's truly serious."

"The Agency seems to think so."

"I know a guy there too," Walker said. "I'll call him." He stood up and offered a hand. "Thanks for coming by."

Burke shook hands and left Walker with a business card. He saw the agent out and returned to his desk, where he picked up the phone and dialed.

The other line picked up after three rings. "Lukavina speaking."

"General Walker, Len."

Lukavina cleared his throat. "Good afternoon, sir. This is a surprise. How are you?"

"The FBI paid me a visit. What's this I hear about Graypoole looking for me?"

"We're not positive. But we're hitting nothing but

dead-ends, sir."

"Len, you don't work for me anymore. Drop the 'sir'."

"Yes, sir. I mean—dammit, General."

Walker laughed. "Dead ends, you said?"

"We think it's Graypoole's kid reviving the organization."

"Okay."

"We're having a hard time getting a fix on him. You and some others may be a target. We need to take precautions."

"I'll make my own arrangements with my people here," Walker said. "I appreciate the tip. If I hear anything—"

"Thank you, sir."

The General didn't bother to correct him. "Surely you have some good news, somewhere?"

"Steve Dane is on the job. He's had first-contact with the enemy so we officially hired him."

Walker laughed. "You mean the Agency had no choice but to hire him. He was going to go after them anyway."

"Correct, General."

"He'll either find answers or cause an international incident."

Dane and the General went back several years, when the Agency participated in joint operations with Walker's special forces team. The only thing Walker didn't like about Dane's personality was his independent nature and his idea orders were merely suggestions until he thought of a better option.

Lukavina said, "What about a sweep of your house?"

"It's checked once a month. Last check was two weeks ago. It was clean. It's always clean."

"All right. If you need anything, don't hesitate to call me."

"I appreciate you being available, Len."

CHAPTER 13

■——■

One of Steve Dane's biggest disappointments the first time he traveled to Berlin was so much of the food available had been Americanized. You could get the same burgers and steaks in Berlin as you could in New York City. Dane always asserted he didn't travel to new places to repeat experiences he could have back home. He traveled to new places to experience new things, including food, but he had to admit the extra effort spent to find new things often led to other exciting discoveries making such trips more memorable.

Dane and Nina and McConn arrived and checked in at the Hotel Adlon Kempinski.

McConn, who didn't care where they stayed as long as there was a roof and four walls, didn't argue about the opulence he otherwise didn't think they needed, especially once they walked into the two-room suite Dane had secured. The door opened on a wood-paneled entryway, bland despite the polished shine of the wood. Walls, floor—all wood. When they stepped through the connecting archway, the wood vanished in favor of brilliant white walls, matching carpet, and plush furnishings. They were in the Brandenburg Gate Suite, so named because the living room windows overlooked the Gate, and with the curtains open the Gate greeted them.

"Wow," McConn said, hands on hips as he took in the view.

Dane carefully set his keys and wallet on the table to the left of the archway before lugging both his suitcases and Nina's into the bedroom.

"When does Stone get here?" McConn said.

Dane checked his watch. "Should be any minute."

Devlin Stone, like McConn, was also a former member of the 30-30 Battalion who now worked as an arms dealer and smuggler. He might have gone for the seedier side of the secret world of espionage and crime, but Devlin Stone was a good man to have on his side.

Lukavina had phoned during the flight to confirm the DCI wanted Dane and his crew on the job and accepted their terms of service, ie: *"Thanks for working for free, Steve. Your country appreciates it."* All it meant in the long run was Dane had access to Agency support and back-up should he require more than his crew to handle the Graypoole situation.

Somebody knocked on the door.

"Speak of the devil."

Nina and McConn remained by the windows while Dane answered the door.

Devlin Stone was the opposite of McConn. They were about the same height, but Devlin had shorter hair, his frame a little leaner; he didn't dress as fancy as Dane but his jeans had a designer label and the black shirt looked like silk.

"Greetings," Stone said. He entered carrying a large case and banged it against the doorway.

"Can we try not to break anything?" Dane said.

"It's fine," Stone said. He placed the case near a couch. "What kind of fun are we having today?"

"We'll talk about it over dinner," Dane said. "What's in the case?"

"Oh, you know. Usual toys. HK sub guns, ammo, few other things."

"I'm not eating at the place downstairs," McConn said. "A sign in front says the special is goose liver."

"They probably won't let you in without a tie," Stone said.

"Never happen," McConn said.

"Don't worry because I got the perfect place in mind," Dane told them.

A tavern around the corner. They sat in a booth in a back corner in the darkened place, which was packed wall-to-wall, loud people, loud music. They could talk business while they gorged on brats, baked ribs and sauerkraut and drank a ton of beer.

Dane didn't spend the whole meal talking about business but gave a general outline of their goals.

"Nina and me will watch the front. I want to see first-hand what the guards do with their day. I'm sure Mueller has some sort of escape route out the back, so Dev and Todd, that's your job. See if you can find it."

"What about the girlfriend?" Stone said.

"We'll pick up her trail after we see the cabin."

"When?" McConn said.

"First thing in the morning so don't stay up too late."

Dane downed what remained of his beer and noticed the pitcher in the center of the table was empty.

"Who's getting the next round?" he said.

Dane awoke before the others, showered and shaved and put on his suit, selecting a red tie. Slipping out of the room, he went down to the lobby for the continental breakfast. He ate three bear claws and drank a cup of green tea while watching the morning news on a corner widescreen, then wandered outside, exploring the property for a place to light a cigar. He found a grassy area overlooking part of the city, the Brandenburg Gate visible. He clipped the end of his Man O' War and set the tip on fire.

The morning chill didn't bother him as he watched the busy street and counted the clouds. He wondered what it would be like at Mueller's cabin. The prospect of action filled him with energy, but the sight of Berlin also made him reflective. There was nothing happening in Berlin not also happening all over the world, but few places affected him the way Germany did. The country had a rich history and proud people, but still suffered from the black eye of the Nazis and, to a lesser extent, the shame of the Wall.

He'd been fourteen when the Berlin Wall came down. His father, a career army intelligence officer who later joined the CIA, had handed him a chunk of the wall on his fifteenth birthday. A souvenir. He remembered examining the hunk of concrete and thought perhaps the world would now be safe from nuclear annihilation. Just what every fifteen-year-old was thinking. The memory always made him laugh. He should have been paying more attention to girls or cars. The irony was the threat of global destruction still existed. It never went away. Only the potential perpetrators changed. Old enemies were now friends; old allies were now enemies; but the struggle for survival continued.

He and Nina and McConn had passed one of the still-existing sections of the wall on their way to the hotel, the slab covered with defiant graffiti. He never failed to consider those who died trying to get over. Freedom was worth the risk and too many paid dearly. Freedom had an allure those born to it didn't understand, those who lived free because somebody else died. Until you've had to fight for the right to exist, you don't truly appreciate it. Two generations after the fall of the wall, Dane wasn't sure anybody did any longer, except for a small minority. Everybody else wanted to keep up with the Kardashians. Girls and cars all over again. Had anything really changed?

Dane puffed on his cigar. He supposed it wasn't all bad. The human condition kept him employed. If the global population suddenly understood the point, he'd have to go string tennis rackets to keep busy and he wasn't sure he was coordinated enough. Or maybe he'd buy a taco truck and set up business on a beach. He had a feeling he'd never have to find out.

An hour later, Dane put the cigar butt in an ashtray near the back exit and took the elevator back to the suite. Time to get the troops organized.

CHAPTER 14

———■———

Nina wasn't happy.

"I wonder what our dry-cleaning bill will be," Nina said.

She lay next to Dane on the muddy ground almost two miles from Mueller's cabin. The ground was soft, the wet dirt applying itself to their dark clothes and camouflaged coats. Some fog still hung above the ground, helping with their cover, since the spindly trees offered so little protection.

Dane examined the front of the cabin through a pair of binoculars.

"Are you listening to me?"

"No," Dane said.

"You're impossible."

"We're not keeping the clothes, dear," he said.

"Well maybe you like looking like a mess but I have standards."

"Nuts. You sleep with me."

She opened her mouth to reply but words suddenly failed her. Instead she said, "What do you see?"

"A cabin."

"I know *that*. What's going on at the cabin?"

"Mueller's two mercenaries stepped out. They're still on the porch. Now one is pointing what looks like a remote at the driveway. The other guy is going down the steps and walking around the perimeter."

Dane lowered the binoculars. He frowned.

"Let me see," she said.

Dane passed her the binoculars.

One of the guards still stood on the porch, while the second was walking a pattern away from the house, going deeper into the surrounding forest, the thin trees not helping him blend in much either. His gray coat did make him vanish in the fog for brief moments. Presently the guard stopped, bent down and used a tool to dig into the dirt.

She described the action to Dane, who said nothing.

The activity took her mind off the conditions in which they currently found themselves. The mud wasn't only sticking to her clothes. She swore she could feel it burrowing through the fabric and into her skin and there was Steve acting as if he was in his natural element.

Sometimes covert operations really sucked. But she certainly wasn't going to stay at the hotel while the boys had all the fun.

The guard removed a black circular object and unscrewed the top, lifting the lid far enough to reach his right hand inside.

"It's a land mine," Nina said. "Making some sort of adjustment."

The guard reburied the mine and followed the same pattern back to the cabin.

"The mines have been diffused and he's still not walking over the other ones," she said.

"Uh-huh."

The guard stepped back onto the porch and the other guard pointed the remote at the ground once again.

Nina lowered the binoculars.

"Instead of trip-wires," she said, "they activate and deactivate land mines with a remote."

"Okay."

"Which means a straight approach is probably out of the question."

"I concur."

Footsteps thumped off to their left. Nina reached for her S&W while Dane remained calm. Todd McConn and Devlin Stone broke through the fog and dropped flat next to them.

"How'd it go?" Dane said as the pair caught their breaths.

"The ground starts to slope about a quarter mile away," McConn said. "We found a cave with an SUV parked inside."

Dane described the remote-controlled mines.

"We can raid the place," he said, "but we might get blown up before we reach the front door. Whoever is left might have a chance, but then Mueller's going to run for the cave."

"There's still the girlfriend," McConn said.

"There certainly is," Dane said.

"I bet they turn off the land mines when she shows up," Nina said.

Dane smiled at her. "Darling, you're brilliant."

"You're only now realizing this?"

"Back to the car," Dane said. The four quickly left the area.

The sign out front read SO-13.

"He named the bar after the anti-terror unit of the British police?" Nina said.

"Who says terrorists don't have a sense of humor?" Dane said.

They sat in a rented BMW halfway down the block from the bar owned by Mueller's buddy, Armand Wulf. McConn and Stone had been inside for almost an hour. Dane let more time tick by and then he and Nina crossed the busy street. He held the door for her and they went inside.

There was none of the thumb-bump-bump music Dane expected. The bar actually had a relaxed atmosphere, was well-lighted and only the mutters of conversation filled the space. Dane spotted McConn and Stone at the bar. They found a corner table. An older waitress came over. Dane ordered a beer while Nina asked for vodka.

Ceiling fans fought against the mass of body heat but did little to alter the sense of Dane's claustrophobia. He sat with his back to the wall while Nina was exposed. If she found it discomforting, she didn't say.

"See any of our friends?"

"Mueller's buddy is behind the bar."

Armand Wulf, a tall and dark-haired fellow, filled drink orders.

Dane's eyes wandered to a door marked Authorized Personnel Only. It probably led to the upstairs loft where Mueller's mercenaries stayed, but near the bar, at a small table, sat a man in black talking to a blonde-haired woman.

"Over by the door," Dane said.

"Where's the other?"

"Not sure."

The waitress returned with the drinks. Dane touched his bottle against the rim of Nina's glass and they took a drink.

"What's your idea?"

"Ask Lukavina to arrange a raid on this place."

"Can he do that quickly?"

"I'm sure he can. Wulf may be worth talking to and we can confirm he's indeed here."

"We'd have to time the raid for when Mueller's girl-friend shows up."

Dane smiled.

Back at the hotel later, Dane and Nina passed a bottle of vodka back and forth while Dane called Lukavina.

He explained about the bar and said, "I'm sure Wulf is somewhere in your files."

"I'll have a look."

"I need you to coordinate a raid with the Berlin police. We need Wulf and the two mercs off the street."

"When were you thinking?"

"We have two days."

"Cutting it close."

"We only have one shot at this, Len."

"I'll get back to you."

CHAPTER 15

■———■

Lanka Kobevko loaded the last of the groceries into the trunk of her Audi. She still had time to get her hair done before picking up Macedo and Storey for the drive to the cabin.

Her slender fingers gripped the steering wheel as she drove through traffic, a light jacket over a blue top and leather boots coming halfway up her jeans. At six feet she was taller than Mueller, model-skinny, with long legs. The wheel was tilted up as far as it could go to keep her from banging her knees getting in and out of the car.

Later in the evening, her formerly straight hair curled with blonde highlights, she made a right turn and started to pull over in front of SO-13, but then slammed the brakes.

Halfway down the street, police units with flashing cherry lights blocked the way. A large crowd had gathered around the bar. Two officers led Armand Wulf into a van. Macedo and Storey were already in the back, shackled to a bench seat. The cops loaded Wulf into the back and closed the double-doors.

Lanka reversed and executed a quick U-turn, digging blindly into the purse on the passenger seat for her cell phone. She found the phone and started to dial, but the phone slipped from her fingers as she slammed the brakes again. A black BMW blocked her. The rear doors opened and two men with automatic weapons jumped out and ran to her car. She locked the doors. One ordered her to open up. She refused. The man bashed the glass. She barely had time to cover her face as shards rained around her. Lanka struck at the man's hand as he reached in and pressed the power lock button, but the blow did nothing to stop him. The man's partner jumped into the back seat. The first man joined him. The muzzle of the man's weapon dug into her neck.

"Drive," the man said, his breath hot on her right cheek.

Dane reversed the BMW to let the Audi go by with Stone and McConn in the back seat.

He fell in line behind the Audi.

Lukavina and the Berlin police had worked fast, indeed.

The route was familiar by now, even with the sun down.

At the halfway point, Dane flashed his lights. The Audi pulled over after a moment. Dane sped by. The Audi pulled back onto the road but the car grew smaller in the rearview as Dane accelerated away.

"Drive normally and you won't get hurt," Stone said. "And keep those hands where I can see them."

"If I don't?" Lanka said.

"I'll kill you. We don't need you, honey."

McConn had grabbed her purse from the passenger seat and placed it on the back seat between him and Stone. They never let her forget the Heckler & Koch MP5Ks they held, the compact submachine guns and their narrow snouts a reminder of the threat.

She drove at moderate speed, both hands on the wheel, breathing heavily. "Hans won't like this."

"He won't have time to complain."

"You're going to kill him?"

"We just want to talk, Lanka."

She flashed a startled look at the rearview. "How do you know who I am?"

"Honey, we know what you had for breakfast."

She forced a laugh. "Tell me."

"Bagel and cream cheese, black coffee."

She didn't force a second laugh.

Hans Mueller dialed the bar but nobody answered.

Lanka was never late. Tonight, she was. By ten minutes.

He tried her cell phone for the third time. Still no answer there, either.

He stepped out on the porch and looked down the length of the driveway to the road beyond. Without a coat, the evening chill bit into his skin. He supposed traffic was to blame, but after San Francisco he was quite keyed up. Had she been intercepted?

Movement to his right. One of his mercenaries, the man's thick coat stopping above his knees. They nodded at each other.

"Looking forward to a few days off?" Mueller said. At least his voice didn't shake.

"Yes, sir," the merc replied. He had his weapon slung across his back.

"Shouldn't be long now," Mueller said. He turned to the road again. When he saw a pair of headlights breaking through the gloom of the forest, he let out a relaxed sigh.

The front door opened and the second mercenary guard stepped out.

The headlights bounced as the car turned off the pavement and then grew in size as the Audi approached.

Mueller swallowed. Took a deep breath. Willed himself to relax. But something wasn't right. She shouldn't have been delayed. Or she should have called.

The Audi stopped at the edge of the driveway. Right where she should have stopped. Somebody who didn't know about the mines wouldn't have stopped.

But still. . .

The mercenary in the long coat reached for the remote control in one pocket. He pulled it out.

"Don't," Mueller said.

The mercenary froze with a questioning look on his face.

Mueller watched the car. It sat still, engine purring. No movement inside. With the lights in his face, he couldn't see the interior.

Presently a head stuck out of the driver's window. "Hans!"

Lanka's voice.

"Okay," Mueller said.

The mercenary pointed the remote at the driveway and clicked a button.

Mueller motioned the Audi forward.

The Audi started to roll, but jerked to a stop, Lanka letting out a howling scream as she bolted from the car.

"Lanka!"

She shouted at Mueller to shoot the car and ran for the tree line.

"Lanka, no!"

The woman crossed through the tree line and then a

burst of SMG fire split open her back. Lanka was dead before she hit the ground.

Mueller fell to his knees and screamed. The mercenaries raised their weapons. Stone and McConn leaned out the back windows and opened fire. The HKs sounded like buzz-saws. The 9mm stingers chewed through the porch railing, shards of wood exploding everywhere. Some of the shots slammed into one of the mercs, cutting him down. He fell against Mueller. The bomb-maker fell from the weight of the dead man, rolling the body of him. The second merc returned fire, shuffling to the far end of the porch.

Mueller grabbed the dead man's gun and fired into the car, shattering the windshield. The trunk popped open. The shooters were slipping out through the rear seat to take cover at the bumper. One of them extended his weapon around the fender. Mueller dropped and rolled right as the rounds chewed up the spot where he'd been. He shouted at the surviving mercenary guard. "Reactivate the mines! Do it now!" He fired on the car as the merc took out the remote and pointed it at the driveway.

CHAPTER 16

———◼———

McConn fired a burst around the left fender, dropping back to cover as Mueller returned fire.

"Run!" he shouted.

Stone didn't argue. They knew either side of the driveway was mined, so Stone did the obvious. He broke into a sprint away from the Audi, heading for the frontage road. McConn fired out his magazine, Mueller and the merc staying low as his salvo rocked the porch and reloaded. Then the earth erupted in a trio of blasts, lifting the Audi off the ground. The force of the blast pulled McConn off his feet and threw him forward. Parts of the car hissed by, flaming bits of shrapnel striking McConn in the back. He scrambled up and kept running. Stone reached the road and fired off a few bursts of covering fire, but the explosion and flames now covering the front of the house blocked their sight of Mueller and the surviving guard.

McConn reloaded his HK. His camo clothing was torn in spots.

"I want to go after them," Stone said.

"And risk the mines?"

"I know, I know."

"Mueller will run for the cave. Come on."

They started running back along the road to where Dane and Nina had left the BMW.

Dane started to rise when he heard the explosion, but Nina put a hand on his shoulder. "They're fine."

More crackling gunfire indicated the fight wasn't over. But then the echo of the shots faded.

Dane clutched his .45 while Nina cradled one of Stone's HKs. A breeze made the branches around them move a little; then they heard pounding footsteps accompanied by huffing and puffing.

Dane and Nina crouched behind a fallen tree trunk, which was perched on the slope about fifteen yards from Mueller's cave. The Ford Explorer inside the cave was set up for immediate departure, with the keys tucked above the driver's side visor. Dane had lifted the hood and yanked off the cylinder coil packs so no matter what, Mueller wasn't going anywhere.

When Mueller and a surviving mercenary guard started down the slope, Dane and Nina tensed, waiting until they were closer. As Mueller reached the cave and put out a hand to guide himself around to the front, Nina triggered a burst from the HK. The salvo cut through the mercenary, splattering Mueller's clothes with blood and sent the merc tumbling down the slope. His body smacked into a tree. Mueller spun around like a top as Dane's .45 slug blasted through his left shoulder. The bomber skidded to a stop halfway to the trunk. Dane and Nina leaped over and ran to the German.

Mueller glared at them through pain-filled eyes, the

blood from his shoulder mixing with the spatter from his guard, the front of his clothes a wet, sticky red. He clawed inside his coat with his right hand, grunting. Dane leveled the .45 at him.

"Show me your hand!"

"See it like this!" Mueller yanked out a pistol.

Dane fired once. The back of Mueller's head exploded, the bullet kicking up a geyser of dirt as it exited his skull and as Mueller's body jerked with one last spasm, the pistol fired. The bullet whistled past Nina's left elbow and burrowed into the tree trunk.

Dane cursed. He knelt beside Mueller's body and ripped open the coat, searching the interior pockets. He found a cell phone.

"Let's see what we can find in the house," he said. Nina followed him up the slope.

Dane paced in the bedroom of the hotel suite, cell phone to his ear. It felt good to be out of his combat garb and back in normal clothes and he felt a sense of accomplishment and satisfaction with the death of Hans Mueller. But Mueller wasn't the end of the mission.

He was only the beginning. His death only partially avenged San Francisco. And while shooting Mueller might have been satisfying, any future leads had died with him. Dane currently had nothing further to go on. He needed Lukavina to provide a clue. He was glad for the access to Agency resources, something he only had because Lukavina convinced the DCI to bring Dane officially into the investigation.

Because he had no plans to slow his assault.

He had left the curtains closed. He didn't think anybody

would try sniping at him from the top of the Brandenburg Gate, but he wasn't taking any chances.

The others were in the living room eating off the sample platters delivered by room service containing a variety of fried items Dane had no interest in consuming.

The CIA man finally picked up the other line.

"We blew it," Dane said.

"Tell me."

Dane related the story.

"We still have Mueller's helpers," Lukavina said. "It's not all bad."

"They may not know much. The phone I found was a burner, nothing there except numbers McConn says reroute a hundred ways."

"Nothing in the house?"

"It was clean. I mean *clean*, Len. I've never seen a place so spotless."

"Even the bathroom?"

"You know what I mean. Mueller's tradecraft was top notch."

"We'll work on the helpers, but I still have tasks for you."

"Go ahead."

"I've been in touch with General Walker and he has his security squared away, but there's somebody else you should go see. The informant who helped us nail Gray-poole Senior is at risk. Malek Kader is the man's name. We can't reach him."

"Is he dead?"

"I don't think so. Kader was a valuable asset. Junior would gloat same as he did about San Francisco. I'll forward the information to your cell. Get to him ASAP."

Dane felt a surge of excited energy rush through his

body. The first round had been a bust, but the second might prove fruitful.

"I'll brief my people as soon as your intel arrives, Len."

"It's on the way."

Lukavina parked the government sedan curbside and exited the vehicle. The streetlamps lit the cul-de-sac well; crickets filled the night.

A man in civilian clothes with a USGI crew cut answered the door. He wore a pistol on his hip.

"Lukavina," the CIA man said. "I'm expected."

The army man asked for Lukavina's ID, which the CIA man provided, along with a business card starting he worked for the Smithsonian Institute, which was part of his cover. CIA employees didn't carry badges or go around announcing themselves.

The soldier confirmed the appointment via radio with somebody inside, then stepped back to let Lukavina enter the house. He followed behind Lukavina and shut the door and told the CIA man to wait. The Marine retrieved General Walker from the family room and he came out to greet Lukavina.

"We're in the middle of packing, Len," Walker said.

"I need to ask you what it would take to cancel the trip, General."

Walker frowned. His wife stuck her head into the room, mouth open, unblinking. Walker guided Lukavina into the study.

"Let's talk about this."

Walker shut the door.

CHAPTER 17

━━━●━━━

It was a small office with only the basics. Desk with computer near a wall covered with pictures of his daughters from birth to adulthood. The bookcase on the other side of the room contained not books but memorabilia from Walker's career. The floor needed cleaning. It was worn from many steps and a dirty path wound its way from the entryway to Walker's desk.

He did not offer Lukavina a chair or a drink and leaned against the front of his desk. Lukavina stood before him. "Did something go wrong in Germany?"

"Mueller is dead. But we didn't find any leads to Graypoole."

"You're assuming he's going to target me."

"It makes sense."

"What makes sense isn't always true."

"General, you'll be overseas. No protection. There will be a target on your back the whole time."

"But if I stay here?"

"Under guard, until we have the situation under control, we think you'll be much safer."

"I can't exactly get a refund on this trip, you know."

"You're going to argue because of the money?"

"My family hasn't had—" Walker stopped. He let out a breath and folded his arms. He looked past Lukavina for a few moments, then: "Give me a percentage. How sure are you I'm a target?"

"Eighty percent. General, you were in charge of the team sent to kill Graypoole's father. You *know* I'm right."

"My family, too?"

"You should all be in one central location until—"

"Right, right, until the situation is under control. I've been in your spot more than once, Len, I know the drill. You know how it is."

"I understand, sir."

"What did I tell you—never mind."

The two men watched each other a moment.

The General said, "I have one CID man in the house, whom you met at the door, and two more down the block in a van. My wife is already nervous enough with the fellow in the house being here."

"I suggest we move you and your family to a safe house or even The Farm, General."

"Help yourself to a drink, Len." Walker moved away from the desk. "I have to talk to my wife." He left the study, closing the door quietly behind him.

Lukavina didn't want a drink. He sat down instead. Then he stood up and moved to the window. He couldn't see much of the yard since it was dark out, but he stared anyway.

He had tried to be optimistic about Germany and the death of Mueller, but Mueller's helpers hadn't provided any further information. Armand Wulf and the other captured mercenaries knew nothing about Mueller's connection to Graypoole. They were only hired hands working directly

for Mueller and had no contact with their employer's employer, though they knew somebody provided instructions
based on a variety of phone calls. CIA officers in Berlin
were certain Wulf and the mercs were telling the truth and
enhanced interrogation protocols had been withdrawn.

They were still playing catch-up against an opponent
who was several steps ahead, and Lukavina was counting, probably, too much on Steve Dane. Throwing agents
around the world searching for the proverbial needle
wasn't a good idea, either. Even the DCI had agreed. Dane
was their best chance, their literal "blunt instrument" in
dealing with the threat.

Malek Kader, the informant who had proved valuable
in the past, who helped them kill Graypoole Senior, was
their best solid lead, if he was still alive. If he wasn't, there
was still his daughter to talk to. Maybe her father had left
with her a failsafe in case of emergency.

Graypoole the Younger had slipped under the radar
and bashed them over the head before they ever knew he
was close enough to strike. Lukavina had no intention of
getting caught off-guard again. There were too many lives
at stake. Some of them close to him.

Lukavina heard Walker raise his voice a little. Penny
raised her voice in return. He couldn't hear everything
they said. Great. A knock-down drag-out. The drink cart
sat against the bookcase, several bottles of whiskey and
bourbon on display along with spotless glasses.

Maybe he'd fix a drink after all.

Walker shut the door and shook his head at Lukavina.

"I'm not going to be very popular for a while."

Lukavina set his glass down half-finished. "My apologies, General."

"Finish your drink, Len." Walker crossed to his desk and sat down. "So. A safe house?"

Lukavina took the chair in front of Walker's desk after the general gestured to it. "Yes. How long will it take your daughters to get here?"

"Day or two."

"I'll make the arrangements then. We'll move you all at the same time, with your CID team, if you like."

"Sure."

"I wish I had a better solution, General."

"It's only money."

"I have control over discretionary funds, sir. I'm sure I can. . .you know."

Walker laughed. "Can you imagine me accepting such an offer, Len?"

Lukavina shrugged.

"But after the butt-chewing I just got. . .I may take you up on it."

Behnam Rostami paced as the wind hammered.

He moved with his arms folded, only a few feet at a time, taking as much shelter as he could near the outer hanger walls but the wind still rushed by. Wind was important at an airport; the Zurich International Airport had a lot of it, with a ton of open space to make sure it stayed plentiful. The runways and terminal buildings were planted in the country with green scenery surrounding the property. It looked as if they constructed the airport in the middle of a farm and told people not to build anything around it. The private hangar, on the north end of the airport, sat across from the main terminal with runways in between. At this distance, he heard none of the organized chaos inside the terminal. He barely heard the jets parked along the jetways as they fired up their engines.

Rostami stopped and checked his watch. Another five minutes, at least, before Mason Graypoole arrived.

Rostami, a former member of the Iranian Secret Service, had been a close confidant of Graypoole Sr., one of the few to escape the raid that killed the elder. When Mason Graypoole had called, Rostami didn't have to think. A lawyer by trade, he'd avoided exposure and the CIA dragnet, during the original hunt for Graypoole the Elder because his firm provided the necessary cover to stay out of sight. He left the firm behind after receiving the call, turning the Zurich law practice to his partners, calling his departure an "extended sabbatical", and now stood waiting for Graypoole to pick him up in the private jet.

He had concerns. Graypoole, unlike his father before him, was being too flashy. After San Francisco, where he practically announced his guilt, the law enforcement and intelligence agencies of the US would be sniffing for him all over the world. Bragging about the SF bombing had already cost the life of Mueller and they'd lost more than a hired gun. They'd lost Mueller's expertise and connections as well. US intelligence had been humiliated and they would spare no expense in their pursuit of vengeance. He knew how they worked. He'd done the same thing as a secret service agent many times, in many countries, chasing Iran's enemies.

Airliners thundered down the runway at regular intervals, the sounds loud enough to bridge the gap where Rostami stood and he examined every plane, noted every distant chirp of tires. So far, no Graypoole. Had something happened?

Rostami took a deep breath. His car was on the other side of the hanger; he could be gone in no time if events turned sour.

And then a jet smaller than any of the airlines appeared over the runway and touched down with yet another chirp of tires. A white Bombardier Global 7000, one of the most expensive private jets money could buy, very fast, very fancy. Twin engines, raised stabilizers on the tail, low-slung wings with flared tips. The fuselage was the usual tubular shape with a rakish profile in front.

Too much flash.

Rostami picked up the suitcase behind him. The plane taxied off the runway and made the slow forward roll to-ward the private hangers. The whine of the engines grew louder as the pointed nose increased in size, and presently the white and gold plane stopped close enough to the hanger for Rostami to reach out and touch the right wing.

The Iranian walked around the nose. The wind beat at him some more, the bright sun scalding the bald spot on his head. He wasn't quite six feet with worry lines on his face and wrinkled skin around his neck. Graypoole's stewardess, a petite Chinese woman with long black hair and brown eyes, wearing what looked like a vintage Pan Am uniform minus the logo, met him at the fuselage door. She lowered a set of steps and he climbed inside.

CHAPTER 18

■———■

"Welcome aboard," she said, raising the steps and pulling the door shut. "Mr. Graypoole is waiting for you."

Rostami muttered his thanks and proceeded down a narrow passage, the fuselage windows on one side, doors leading to the four rooms on board to his left, the bedroom, game room, TV room and bar. He held his suitcase before him as he cleared the passage into the Global 7000's dining area, a space with dark paneling, beige carpeting and a long dining table. The jet could take ten passengers, but the table only seated six.

Graypoole sat at the table facing a wide screen television mounted on the forward wall. He smiled and raised a glass at Rostami.

"Ben," he said, using the infuriating shortened version of Rostami's name. The Iranian put his suitcase down and leaned across the table to shake hands. The engines outside flared and the plane started moving. Rostami found a chair.

Graypoole gestured at the TV. "I recorded the CNN reports on San Francisco. It's exhilarating, isn't it?"

Rostami ignored the question and watched at the footage without seeing it. He turned to Graypoole. "You know about Mueller?"

"Of course."

"Then you know why I consider it a failure."

"Casualties are a fact of war, Ben."

"And the pair Mueller reported? Dane and Talikova?"

Graypoole made a dismissive gesture with his free hand. "They're mercenaries. The US government would have paid them for Mueller's capture. That's all he was interested in. He won't waste time and his own money chasing us."

"You are mistaken, young man. I'm not sure you're aware of the problem he and Talikova pose."

"Why would they?" Graypoole said. "It'll be a point of pride for the CIA to find us themselves, not hire outsiders."

Rostami regarded the younger man coldly. "We have to be careful or we will suffer the same fate as your father."

"The whole point is to not let that happen," Graypoole said, raising his voice. "We're going to hit them so hard and so fast, we'll be long gone before they get any steam. Hell, they're still trying to figure out where I came from."

Rostami sat back as the plane picked up speed, the ride a little bumpy. Shortly it slowed to a stop. Rostami glanced around the cabin.

Graypoole let out a breath and lowered his voice. "Seattle is underway. Ramos filed his first report this morning."

Rostami nodded.

"And we won't be moving around much longer. I have an appointment in Bahrain, and then we go to the island."

Rostami frowned. "The island is finished?"

"It is. Nobody will look for us there."

"And General Walker?"

"He's covered. I bought a house across the street from

his and put our team there. They've been watching him for months."

"How long have you been planning these operations?"

"Quite some time, Ben. I know what you're thinking, but I've done all I can to prepare for this. I can't stay cooped up any longer. I *will* have my revenge."

Rostami let out a breath. "I suppose this is where I ask for a drink."

Graypoole reached for a panel on the table and pressed a button. The Chinese woman arrived. Rostami asked for what Graypoole was drinking and she departed. Rostami fidgeted in his seat.

"I counseled your father many times throughout the years. I am happy to provide you with the same counsel, which means I must caution you, Mason. The side trip to Bahrain is not safe. Send somebody else."

"I don't disagree. It's a huge risk, but I have to kill Kader myself. If it hadn't been for him, my father would still be alive."

"Mason—"

"It won't take long. We won't even set foot on the ground."

"What?"

"Well, we'll be there long enough to get onto a helicopter." Graypoole grinned. "You can wait with the plane if you'd like."

The cell phone in Graypoole's pocket chirped. He took out the phone and answered. It was a short call and he listened for a moment before only responding with a curt, "Okay." He put the phone away without saying good-bye.

"Walker has cancelled Rome," he said.

"What does that—"

"I don't know." He clenched his jaw and balled a fist.

"You can't have everything."

Rostami took a drink. Graypoole's voice had an edge to it now, a frustrated edge. The same tone his father had displayed when something went wrong, which usually resulted in Graypoole the Elder making mistakes. Mason Graypoole took out the cell phone again and dialed the team watching Walker's house.

"Hit the house. Kill everybody inside."

Graypoole put away the phone and called the steward-ess for a refill.

Rostami stared at him.

"Do you have something to say?" Graypoole said.

Rostami shook his head. "You wouldn't listen anyway."

Ernest Levasseur slipped his phone into a pocket and surveyed the room.

Their surveillance gear occupied most of the living room of the home they used to watch the Walkers, a 3-bed-room, 2-bath single story. A bank of monitors showed the exterior of the Walker house. When they moved in two months earlier to begin watching the family, they had talked about penetrating Walker's standard home security system and slipping into the home to plant cameras and bugs. Then they noticed the CID team arrived to regularly sweep the house for such things, so they nixed the idea. They instead rigged small cameras on the roof of *their* house, which were aimed at the General's and had to settle for quiet visuals of the comings and goings.

Levasseur and his teammates, burly Italians named Gaetano and Cotrone, sat in shifts around the gear. They were also supposed to clean the house in shifts, because the Frenchman refused to live in a pigsty, but as he picked up a discarded Snickers wrapper from along the wall trim, he realized nothing can ever be perfect. Much like the mission.

At least they didn't fail to keep the front lawn mowed. Have to keep up appearances.

Cotrone sat before the monitors watching Levasseur expectantly. Gaetano sat at the kitchen table with a plate of cheesy scrambled eggs.

"Was that Graypoole?" Cotrone said.

"Yes. Change in plans. He wants the whole family gone. We hit the house when the daughters arrive."

"Before they leave?"

"They aren't leaving."

"But the guards. . ."

"I know. Show me where they are."

Levasseur stepped closer to Cotrone as the Italian typed commands. One of the monitors showing the outside of the Walker home rotated until it stopped on a white van parked down the block.

"When will they stop using silly vans," the Frenchman said.

Dishes clinked as Gaetano put his plate in the sink. He came over to join them carrying a folding chair. Their furniture consisted of folding chairs and cots, but at least they had separate rooms.

"I can take the van," Cotrone said, "and have the car running while you two go into the house."

"Are you sure?"

Cotrone swallowed. He was normally a surveillance man, not a shooter. He said, "Yes. I can."

Gaetano said, "I don't like this. We had a good plan."

The original idea had been to shoot the Walkers' car on the way to the airport. The exit of their neighborhood narrowed to two lanes before emptying onto an expressway, a great ambush point.

"We also," Gaetano said, "have a problem with our weapons."

They only had rifles and one submachine gun. The idea had been to shoot out the car's tires with the rifles, then hose the couple inside the car with the submachine gun.

"We have handguns," Cotrone said.

Levasseur nodded. "Gaetano, you'll need the sub-machine gun for the van. Cotrone, we'll have to use the handguns."

Cotrone shook his head.

Levasseur held up the Snickers bar. "To whom does this belong?"

Gaetano snatched it out of Levasseur's hand.

"Keep the place clean, please," Levasseur said as he turned away.

CHAPTER 19

◼━━━━◼

The whine of the engine was barely discernible through the fuselage.

"Extra insulation," Stone explained. "Jet's a little heavier but it sure is quieter."

The four were in Stone's private jet, seated in soft leather chairs in the mostly beige cabin, the jet still climbing. The G-force of the climb pushed them back into the seats.

Dane rotated his seat to glance out the window. They were high enough where he couldn't tell exactly where they were, but they were for sure still within Germany. Below he saw the steeples of village churches breaking through the forest. They looked very small so high up.

Nina sat near Dane, a small table between them. As the plane leveled she said, "We need to get one of these, Steve."

"No way."

"It'll be great."

"Nope."

"But we'll save a ton on baggage fees."

"Pack less."

She scoffed.

The jet was all business. Up front of the cabin was a video screen of about 60-inches. Stone said they had satellite TV should anyone want to watch *Love It or List It*. A small dining table could seat four if they squeezed together and the galley was at the rear, room for one at a time. In between, the chairs lined either side.

"You haul any cargo in this?" Dane said.

"Just me or guests."

"I bet it's perfect for quick hops to Barcelona," Nina said.

"We're *not* buying a jet," Dane said.

Stone visited the galley for a few moments and brought everybody drinks, which were accepted with thanks. Dane took out a cigar and clipped the end.

"Take it to the smoking area, Steve."

Dane frowned. "And where is your smoking area?"

"The left wing."

Dane shook his head. He put the Montecristo back into its container, the container back in his pocket. "Can we put Lukavina's info on the screen?"

"Sure." From an overhead compartment near the dining table, Stone took down a laptop which he plugged into the TV and told Dane to email the Kader file to a specific address. Dane swallowed some Canada Dry and Makers and complied using his smartphone. Stone typed commands and put the picture of Malek Kader on the screen. He was obviously tall, broad chest, shoulders, thick neck. Full head of dark hair, graying goatee. Defiant dark eyes.

Dane rose to talk.

"That's our guy." He consulted his phone. "Lukavina says he was a key man in assassinating Graypoole Senior. Kader organized Graypoole's forces like a real military outfit, battalions to squads to teams and coordinated each group's budget."

"Why did he turn rat?" McConn said.

Dane scrolled through the file.

"His wife died, number one. Then Graypoole blew up a nightclub where twenty-two civilians died. Apparently, Kader got cold feet shortly after. Civilians weren't supposed to be targets."

"What about the daughter?" Nina said.

Stone tapped a key and put Hana Kader on the screen. She had long black hair and dark eyes like her father, but a smaller face, small mouth and nose.

And big brown eyes.

Dane shivered at the sudden flashback the young woman provided but he kept his face straight. How much did she know about her father? Would Graypoole's gun sights find her, too?

"Is she with her father?" Stone said.

"No. London, it says here."

"I hope Lukavina has her covered," Stone said.

"If Graypoole knows Kader sold out his old man—" Nina said.

"Len thinks that's possible."

"—will Junior show up to pull the trigger himself?"

"I think he'd want to," Stone said, the others agreeing.

"Let's say he will," Nina said. "If we time it right—"

"—we can end this before the next bomb goes off," Dane finished. "We *absolutely* need to stop this before Graypoole raises the death toll higher than it already is."

Dane looked out the window across the expanse of ocean with the thirty islands making up Bahrain growing in the distance.

"Ever been there before?" Stone said. He eased into the seat beside Dane's chair.

"No. One of the few places not marked on my passport."

"It's not a bad place, give or take a few things," Stone said. "I've run a lot of stuff through there. Mostly expats and non-Arabs so they're a little more relaxed than other places in this region."

"What are some of the give or take things?" Dane said.

"A lot of foreign workers are trafficked through here," Stone said. "Get their passports taken from them, if they have passports; paid slave wages, indentured servitude, that sort of thing."

Dane shook his head.

"One hell of a grand prix, though," Stone added.

"I'm sure it makes the rest okay."

As they flew over the country, Dane noticed some of the land was full of development, tall buildings and neighborhoods, but other parts had buildings separated by blocks of open lots, full of the burnt-orange sand that made up the landscape.

Nina came up behind him and kneaded his shoulders.

"At least we're here in winter," Nina said.

The sun blazed in the clear blue sky.

"Winter in Bahrain is like summer in California, minus the dust storms," Stone said.

The jet continued across the length of the country, heading for Bahrain International Airport. The airport was located in Muharraq, an island about four miles northeast of Manama, the capital. They would need to cross the bin Salman Causeway to reach the capital, easily doable by taxi, if they could find an honest cabbie.

"What does that mean?"

"Sometimes the meters are rigged."

"This place keeps getting better," Dane said. He exchanged a frown with Nina.

The jet landed and it took forever to get through customs. Because they used a private jet, they were ushered into a private room where their bags were thoroughly searched. Another crew searched the plane itself. None of them worried about weapons being found. Stone had compartments built under the carpet where they'd stashed the hardware. The searchers would need an X-ray machine to see the compartments. It only meant a delay in getting to their weapons and gear. After the search was done, the pilot would taxi the plane into a private hanger off the main terminal and once parked, they could access the plane when they wanted.

After clearing customs and collecting weapons, they went out front and Stone started down a cab line. The first cab had a broken meter and quoted a higher rate than the trip to their hotel warranted. Stone passed. The next cab had no meter but the driver said they could negotiate. Stone passed. The next cab had a fully functioning meter, the dark-haired driver young and eager to serve. The driver was shorter than both of them, wore large-framed glasses and kept asking about America. Everybody climbed into the cab. Dane took the front seat with the others squeezing into the back.

The cab left the airport following Airport Avenue. Blue ocean stretched to infinity on the right, the growing capital city of Manama in the distance. To the left, more burnt-orange land with buildings scattered here and there. When the car went up the slight incline of the Shaikh Bin Salman Causeway, Dane gazed out at the shipping channel below filled with cargo ships. The channel continued to the south.

Traffic was light, the roads very smooth. Dane noted

no bumps. Roads in America weren't as good. The driver turned onto the King Faisal Highway, following a sweeping curve into the capital city. A bright yellow Lamborghini zoomed past them. A Gallardo. Dane would have been more impressed if it had been the current model.

Dane watched the people on the street. The Bahrainis were easy to spot. Most of them wore traditional robed garb, but others sported western clothes. He found it odd this Islamic country could be so established in its religion, but open to western influence. The economy had a much to do with it, Stone explained. A lot of Filipinos and whites were mixed in with the sidewalk traffic. Without them the country didn't function, so, yeah, wear the Levis and Me-tallica T-shirt. Domes of mosques were still visible in the skyline, though. In another striking contrast, Dane counted at least two McDonalds and one KFC. Even on the other side of the world, you can get a Big Mac. Dane wasn't sure if the Golden Arches was good for diplomacy or not, but based on the crowds inside, nobody was complaining.

The Financial Harbor loomed ahead, two tall buildings stretching as high as the sky. They were the bookends of a smaller cluster of buildings in between.

The King Abdullah ibn Al-Hassain Avenue led to the Ritz-Carlton and here was Bahrain's western influence all in one spot, an oasis in a burnt-orange sea. The palace-like structure stood tall and white against the backdrop of blue sky and sand, surrounded not only by parking lots but a man-made lake, with more sand (of the beach variety) circling the perimeter of the water.

"Steve, I think we have a tail," McConn said. "Two cars, very nice BMWs.""They're not going to try anything on the street," Stone said.

"You sure?" Dane said.

"Well. . ."

"Thought so."

The driver said, "What is going on?"

"Can you *really* drive this car?"

"What do you—"

"Steve!" Nina shouted.

The first of the BMWs shot past the driver's side of the taxi, cut in front and slammed its brakes. The driver let out a yell and stomped his own, the taxi screeching to a halt mere inches from the BMWs bumper. Everybody strained against their seat belts, snapping back once the car stopped. Dane looked back. The other BMW had stopped directly behind the taxi. They were boxed in.

CHAPTER 20

——◼——◼——

Two men climbed out of the back BMW. Other cars honked and moved around, more honking and shaking fists as the annoyed drivers passed, but the two men in suits who approached the taxi paid no mind. Each wore sunglasses, one a dark suit while the other wore tan. The man in tan took out a pistol and stood near the passenger window aiming at Stone's face while the other man tapped on the driver's window.

"What do I do?" the driver said.

"Roll down the window," Dane said.

The driver complied. The window whispered down.

"You will come with us," the man said.

"Or what?"

"Or what do you think?" the man said.

"Steve—"

"Not now, Nina. I think we should do what he says." Dane took out his wallet and removed some bills. He handed the cabbie several of them.

With horns continuously honking around them and the back-up growing, Dane and his crew were split into each of the BMWs. When the BMWs cleared out, traffic still couldn't resume its normal pace, because the taxi driver sat behind the wheel with his hands shaking.

Dane rode in the back seat with Nina beside him. The driver and passenger up front said nothing to them. The second BMW stayed a few car lengths behind. They weren't bound, nobody held a gun on them, and there was no indication they were in enemy hands.

Dane and Nina raised eyebrows at each other.

"Where are we going?" he said.

"No talking."

"Either you tell me or I can't promise my lady friend won't vomit all over this plush leather back seat."

"I get car sick," Nina said. "My Dramamine is in my suitcase."

The passenger turned around, his sunglasses preventing them from seeing his eyes but there was no doubt he was less than pleased.

"Stop. Talking. We're taking you to Kader."

"Who?"

"Malek Kader. The man you came to see."

"How in the world—"

"We have people everywhere, Mr. Dane. You may not know him, but he knows you." The man faced forward again.

Dane and Nina exchanged another eyebrow raise.

"I think I can keep from vomiting for a while," she said.

He patted her leg.

Dane checked behind them. The other BMW with Stone and McConn remained only a few cars back.

The driver turned off the highway and onto a two-lane road leading to what looked like an unfinished hotel. The Alrays Suites, a tall cream-white building with some side structures to one side resembling office space. A dirt lot surrounded the structure, and the driver turned off the pavement onto the dirt. The car rocked side-to-side, the dust cloud billowing around the windows.

The BMW circled the side buildings and aimed for a covered parking area near the rear entrance. The second BMW pulled up alongside. Everybody climbed out before the dust cleared. Nina coughed, waved a hand in front of her face and brushed the front of her shirt and jeans.

"These were clean clothes when the day started," she said.

"Tell me about it," Dane said, noting the dust clinging to his blazer.

"Inside," Sunglasses said. The four men flanked Dane, Nina and Stone and McConn as they walked toward the back entrance.

Dane looked over his shoulder at his compatriots. "You two all right?"

"Maybe a battered ego," Stone said.

"Or two," McConn added.

"We'll live," Dane said.

"Says you," Nina said.

Sunglasses scowled.

"Should we stop talking?" Dane said.

Sunglasses made no reply.

The inside of the structure only confirmed Dane's opinion the building wasn't finished. The walls were up but wiring stuck out of spots in the wall for fixtures. There was no sign of continued construction. No workbenches, scaffolding, or anything else associated with such activity.

Everything was swept clean and spotless.

Sunglasses stopped them at an elevator and dismissed the two men who had brought McConn and Stone. Sunglasses and his partner pushed Dane, Nina, McConn and Stone into the elevator and joined them. The doors slid shut.

Sunglasses pressed the button for the 24th floor and the elevator car rumbled upward. The walls of the car were gray, scratched and unremarkable. Dane couldn't help but wonder where they were going. He glanced at McConn and Stone. Their stoic faces betrayed nothing, but he knew they were imagining possible scenarios and how to overcome them. He should have been doing the same but preferred to improvise. The ghosts of battles past also whispered reassurance.

The doors opened on the living room of a well-furnished penthouse suite.

A tall man with a thick chest, graying goatee and full head of black hair stood before them.

"Welcome, Mr. Dane, Miss Talikova. Who are your associates?"

"Mr. Kader, I presume?" Dane said as they exited. The doors whispered closed.

"Yes, yes, I've been eager to see you since my people spotted you at the airport."

Kader offered an enthusiastic handshake to Dane and his people. Dane introduced McConn and Stone. Kader told Sunglasses and his partner to stay by the elevator. Kader brought his four guests deeper into the living room; the suite was the exact opposite of everything downstairs.

"I own the building," Kader explained. "Once the trouble with Graypoole started I had everyone clear out."

The furnishings were top-notch, the carpet very soft,

silk curtains, paintings. Dane recognized what looked like an original Rembrandt. The perfect inner sanctum. A vinyl record player and hi-fi system occupied one wall. Dane eyed it with interest.

"I collect old jazz records," Kader said. "No CDs or MP3s for me."

He took them to a table filled with food. Chicken and beef kebabs, grilled vegetables, rice, pitchers of ice water with lemon slices. Kader sat everybody, took the head of the table with Dane to his right. A dark-haired waiter in a white mess jacket began distributing the food and pouring water. His jacket fell open as he filled Dane's glass. Dane spotted a Beretta pistol hanging under the man's right arm.

Dane said, "We're glad you're still alive."

"So am I," Kader said. "Please, start eating, don't wait for me. Mr. Dane, I had to drop out of sight. You can explain to the CIA. I'm sure they will understand."

"You've been expecting somebody to come find you."

"My security people had the airport covered 24/7, as you saw. You were photographed coming off the plane."

"Uh-huh. This beef is delightful," Dane said, chewing some more. It wasn't overcooked; perfectly juicy; with the right amount of seasoning.

"You have questions for me," Kader said.

"The Graypoole kid has Langley stumped and we lost a lead in Germany," Dane said. "What do you know?"

Kader shrugged and ate part of a bell pepper. "I'm as surprised as Langley. Mason Graypoole was never a consideration. His father had no contact with him. His mother *forbade* contact. His father always knew where he was, had people checking on him. He called the boy his secret weapon and hoped he might someday join the cause."

"He's reached out to his father's old operatives,"

Dane said.

Kader nodded.

"What do you have on them we might be able to use?"

"I wouldn't know where to start," Kader said. "I put all of the information on the computer so I wouldn't have to remember."

"Then we can have that?"

"Yes. But it's not here. I don't mean at this safe house, but in Bahrain. My daughter has the thumb drive everything is stored on."

"She's still in London?"

"Exactly. She's under guard. I own a flower shop on Bedfordbury and Bedford. She's there."

"I sent two of my best men to keep her safe," Kader continued. "She is not happy, complains like her mother, but she's waiting for you. When you arrive, tell the clerk 'Crash Dive'."

"We'll stay long enough to get you out of the country."

Kader held up a hand. "I'm safe here, Mr. Dane. Nobody knows about this place. It's why I built it."

"I don't think it's wise."

"This is my home, Mr. Dane."

Nina put down her kebab. "Spare us the whining," she said. "Once Graypoole is dead you can come back. All you'll have to do is dust the place."

Kader looked at Nina with wide eyes and then frowned at Dane.

"She is your—"

"Better half," Dane said.

Kader sipped some water and eased back in the chair. A few moments ticked by.

CHAPTER 21

◼—◼

"I think you're right," Kader said. "How long will it take to arrange transport?"

Dane wiped his mouth and stood up. "We have a plane waiting."

Dane took out his cell and wandered over to the hi-fi. Three leather chairs and a coffee table sat before the five-foot high speakers. He flipped through the record collection as he waited for Lukavina to answer.

"I hope you have good news," Lukavina said.

"Kader's alive," Dane began, and started to fill him in. He turned. Nina, McConn, and Stone still sat at the table while Kader had left to stand in front of a wide window looking out over the city.

Tall steel-and-glass buildings reflected the glare of the sun; the ocean in the distance quietly shimmered.

It would be hard for Dane to leave a place like this, too.

He finished the update.

Lukavina said, "When can you be in the air?"

"Within the hour," Dane said. "The fuse is getting short."

"Keep me updated," Lukavina said. He hung up.

Dane started to put his phone away when the whipping rotor blades of a chopper broke through the quiet. The noise got louder.

"Kader—" Dane began.

The chopper dropped down and hovered in front of the window where Kader stood. A glare flashed off the canopy. The chopper rotated to reveal the open side door. A young man, grinning, sat behind a machine gun. The weapon spat flame, the window shattering, Kader crying out and falling as shards of glass coated the carpet.

Dane dropped, Nina and the others hitting the floor, as the machine gun hammered some more. Bullets zipped through the suite, wreaking havoc, destroying the hi-fi, and then the chopper pulled away.

Sunglasses and his partner had their pistols out.

"Get help!" Dane shouted.

Sunglasses turned and shot his partner through the head and swung his pistol to Dane.

Dane dived in front of the nearest chair. Two pistols shots smashed into the wall behind him. He looked up. Sunglasses aimed at the table. Nina and McConn pushed it over, the food and water spilling with a loud crash. Sunglasses sent his next two rounds into the tabletop, splintering the polished wood.

Dane grabbed one of the jazz records and flung it like a Frisbee. The record closed the distance, Sunglasses turning to Dane as the record caught him in the neck. He let out a yell, recoiling back a step.

Dane launched himself off the back of the chair and collided with Sunglasses in a flying tackle.

They smashed against the wall, hot breath from Sunglasses scraping Dane's neck. Dane pounded a one-two combo into the man's torso. Sunglasses grunted, shoving at Dane with his free hand. He brought the butt of his gun down hard against the side of Dane's head.

Dane's vision spun. He collapsed mid-swing, Sunglasses delivering a solid kick to his stomach. Dane stifled a yell and grabbed the other man's ankle as he readied another kick and as he lost his balance, Sunglasses pointed the gun at Dane's face.

A shot crackled. Dane blinked. Something warm and wet splattered on his chest and neck but it wasn't his blood. A bullet had gone through Sunglasses' left eye, the lens gone, the gaping red hole left behind hemorrhaging blood down his jaw to the front of his suit. The exit wound on the side of his head painted the white wall behind with more blood and tissue fragments. Sunglasses teetered a moment and then fell hard.

The waiter, in a basic isosceles stance, lowered his smoking Beretta.

Dane ran to the others, who were clustered around Kader's body.

"He's hurt but still alive," Stone reported. They were on their knees around the man, trying to plug his wounds with cloth napkins, all of which were soaked red.

The waiter exchanged his gun for a cell phone and called for help. He put the phone away and grabbed Dane. "Get to London," he said. "We'll handle this."

"Nice shooting," Dane said.

Dane and his team ran out of there, stepping over the traitor's body. McConn paused to dig through Sunglasses' pockets and found his phone. Nina grabbed the keys to the BMW from the guard Sunglasses had killed.

The elevator doors shut and the car began its descent.

Dane removed his blazer, pulling a handkerchief from the inside pockets. He wiped his face and neck. He regarded the blazer with a sigh and dropped it on the floor.

"Anybody hurt?"

"We're cool," Stone said.

Nina hugged Dane tight.

Downstairs they piled into the first BMW. Dane peeled out of there leaving a billowing dust cloud in their wake.

"So that was Junior," Nina said.

McConn, in the back with Stone, scrolled through the captured cell.

"He sent a text before the shooting, Steve. They know about London."

"How did you crack his password?"

"Do you even have to ask?"

"Doesn't matter if they know," Nina said. "I'd like a chance to even the score."

"Get in line," Dane said.

"Ladies first," she told him.

"You missed."

Mason Graypoole froze as the flight attendant pulled the fuselage door shut. He glanced at her. The look on his face made her quickly pivot and leave the cabin.

The engines spooled up as the pilots prepared to taxi.

Graypoole faced Behnam Rostami as the Iranian lawyer lounged comfortable in a chair.

"What do you mean?"

The plane started to roll.

"You better sit down before you fall over."

"Dammit, Ben—" Graypoole took a seat across from the lawyer. He sat on the edge, leaning toward Rostami, his expression intense.

"Our spotters say Kader survived. Our man inside did

not. Killed by an American."

"I saw four others with Kader."

"Americans. Looking for you."

Rostami needed to be careful. He didn't want the younger man to end up screaming and pacing around; he needed to deliver the lesson the younger man needed to hear calmly. A line had been crossed and there was no turning back.

Graypoole didn't respond. He sat back in the seat, crossed his legs and stared ahead. Rostami did not press him to say anything. As the jet finally took off, the lawyer knew Graypoole would need a few moments to process what he had said.

"And the Americans probably saw my face," Graypoole said.

Rostami raised an eyebrow. He hadn't expected the realization to arrive so quickly.

"They can match you with file photographs and confirm you exist."

Graypoole cleared his throat. He didn't look at Rostami. "What is this cause all about, Mason?"

Graypoole turned sharply. *Now* he looked at the lawyer. "Say that again."

"Your cause. What is it about?"

"Revenge. I told you."

"Why?"

"Because they killed my father. It's up to me to avenge him."

"Where was this sense of devotion when your father was alive?"

Graypoole flinched.

"Tell me, Mason."

Graypoole's shoulders sank. "Maybe that's the reason.

You don't appreciate what you have until it's gone. My mother—"

"Kept you from your father, I remember. It hurt him a great deal. She didn't agree with what he was doing and she didn't want you corrupted by him."

"It wasn't her choice. I wanted to see him. She refused. Then the Americans *truly* took him from me when they put a bullet in his back. I didn't get the chance to know him as I should have, so now I will keep his memory alive, one way or another."

"Your father wasn't the man to take you to baseball games, Mason. He might have shown you how to field strip an AK-47 instead."

Graypoole didn't smile.

"There were certain security protocols in place," Rostami continued, "where such visits would have been difficult anyway. One thing he was glad about was nobody could use you and your mother to get to him. In a way, his gift to you was to keep you safe and out of the line of fire. He'd made his choices. He hoped you'd join him someday, but he didn't think it right to involve you at a young age."

"I learned weapons on my own. I had to."

"Of course. And you've done well. Your goal has been achieved. The Americans will indeed always remember the Graypoole name, but there is something you must understand."

"What?"

"You've begun a journey you cannot return from. Had you kept your identity a secret, used your father's forces as a means to accomplish your goals, you might have survived much longer."

"Why are you speaking in past tense?"

"Because it's only a matter of time now, Mason. They

are going to find you and you, as I, will meet our destiny."

"So be it," Graypoole said.

Rostami sat back with nothing more to say.

The jet flew on.

McConn and Stone dozed as the jet soared toward London. Dane and Nina occupied the same seat but it was a tight fit, with Nina wedged in between Dane and the left side armrest. She sipped from a glass of vodka.

"We're crossing so many time zones," she said, "I don't know what year it is."

Dane smiled and rubbed her leg.

"What's bothering you?" she said.

Dane stared ahead with his jaw tight. "We're one step behind."

"You're getting too involved. Emotionally, I mean."

"You didn't see that girl's face, Nina."

"You're no good to her or any of us if you get killed too."

"I want to shoot the little punk. You didn't see him grin before he shot Kader. He thinks this is a game."

"We've faced worse."

"We have, haven't we?"

"Don't forget the girl," Nina said, "but stay detached. Too much emotion breeds mistakes."

"We've made enough of those already," Dane said.

CHAPTER 22

————◆————

Another airport. Busy Heathrow. Another customs check. Another car rental—a small SUV. The four piled into the vehicle. Stone drove. And this time they pulled over off the airport property to get their weapons from the luggage.

Stone steered along the narrow streets with Dane navigating in the passenger seat via cell phone map. Clouds were thick but only held the threat of rain. The buildings they passed as they entered the neighborhood were either made of brick or stone and wore weathered patina.

"I could go for some shepherd's pie while we're here," McConn said.

"No time," Dane said.

Stone pulled over.

"Wait here," Dane said. He started to get out.

"You'll need me," Nina said. She joined Dane on the sidewalk. They entered the flower shop.

"Don't like my pals?" Dane said.

"She'll feel better with a woman around."

The clerk behind the counter smiled.

"Help you, sir?"

The place was wall-to-wall flowers, an explosion of colors and scents.

Dane said, "Crash Dive."

The clerk said, "We've been expecting you," as he pressed a button under the counter. No buzzer sounded but a door labeled Private popped open on a hydraulic hinge.

"Up the stairs and down the hall," the clerk said.

"Does she know about her father?" Dane said.

"Yes."

"Any word on his condition?"

"None," the clerk said, with a slight shake of his head. "No trouble here, either."

"Okay."

Dane pushed the door open. Nina drew her Smith & Wesson M&P Shield and held it close to her leg.

A light bulb hung from the ceiling and lit the narrow hallway. A set of stairs led to a hallway, and at the end was a door with a pool of light spilling from underneath.

Nina stopped against the wall as Dane continued. He knocked on the door.

A bald man in a dark suit answered. He held a gun very loosely, examined Dane. "Who's the woman?" he said.

"She's with me."

"Put away the piece, chrome dome," Nina said.

The bald man complied and let Dane into the room. He held the door for Nina.

A young woman rushed at them from a corner couch. "What happened to my father?"

She was shorter than she looked in the picture; her dark hair had blonde highlights. Her eyes burned with concern.

"He was alive when we left," Dane said. "I don't know anything more. Neither did the guy downstairs."

"Nobody knows nothing!" Hana Kader said.

"Anything," Nina said.

"Who *are* you two anyway?"

Dane looked at Hana. Her small lips were pressed tightly together, her eyes locked on Nina, breathing steadily. Ready for a fight.

"Hana, look at me."

The girl snapped her attention to Dane. "What?" She couldn't have been more than 25 but seemed mad enough to wrestle a tiger. Her brown eyes stood out the most to him. He had to keep this young woman alive.

Steady. Stay focused.

"Your father said you have information about Graypoole."

"Yeah, so?"

"I need those files."

"They aren't here."

"Will you take us to them?"

"They're at my Swiss bank."

Dane said, "Then you're coming with us."

"What about the people who shot my father?"

Dane checked his watch. "Should be here any time."

"Are you serious?"

"I'm surprised they didn't get here first, considering one of your father's men betrayed him."

She put a hand to her mouth.

"We have to go," Dane said. "Right now."

Hana Kader no longer argued.

Dane wanted to be back in the air without delay.

"No way," Stone said as he drove. "My pilots need rest, Steve."

"We don't have time to wait."

"Can you fly that plane yourself?"

Dane thought a moment. "Okay. We hole up tonight and take off in the morning. Todd, shepherd's pie on me."

"Awesome," McConn said.

They checked into a hotel near Heathrow, two separate rooms. Nina and Hana occupied one. Nina figured some girl time might settle Hana's nerves.

Dane escorted the women to their room, placing their bags on the floor with a grunt of relief. It felt like they had packed the State of Texas.

"Don't stay up too late," Nina said. Dane departed for his room, located further down the dark-walled hallway. Carved wooden arches were set above each door, the number of the room dead-center in each arch.

Dane found McConn and Stone around the table shuffling cards and counting poker chips.

"Where'd you get the kit?" Dane said.

"Gift shop."

There were two king beds. And three of them. A folded cot sat against the dresser. Thin mattress, metal frame. The paint on the wheels was chipped, faded. It didn't look uncomfortable, but it also didn't look very inviting.

"Are we playing for who gets the beds?" Dane turned up the cuffs of his shirt, but only a little. The puckered flesh of his left arm remained covered.

"Exactly," Stone said. He set aside a stack of blues and started counting reds.

Dane fished his cell out of his coat. "One second." He dialed Lukavina and caught the CIA man at home.

"We found the daughter and no trouble," Dane reported. "Her father's files are in a bank in Zurich. But if one of Kader's men told Graypoole where he was hiding, you can bet they know what we know and they aren't far behind."

"When do you leave for Zurich?"

"Tomorrow morning. I'll call you again when we get there."

Dane ended the call.

He approached the table. "I have no intention of sleeping on that cot, boys."

"Dealer's choice," McConn said with a final shuffle of the deck.

The cot really wasn't bad, Dane later decided.

CHAPTER 23

■———■

The Walker daughters arrived in the evening, each in their own car and from what Levasseur could discern based on how each one was greeted at the door, it was a grand reunion and they weren't going to let a cancelled trip ruin their togetherness.

He smiled a little.

The sun went down and the lights went on; a Dominos delivery man arrived with two pizzas. Levasseur guessed nobody wanted to cook.

The Frenchman continued watching the house on the monitors and before midnight the CID agents changed shifts. Two new arrivals replaced the men in the van, and a lone agent took the place of the one in the house.

Levasseur left the monitors to join Gaetano and Cotrone in the kitchen. The two sat at the table oiling their weapons. Levasseur had already prepared his pistol; it hung below his left arm. Cotrone had the only submachine gun, a Heckler & Koch MP-7. He had the parts disassembled and spread neatly on a layer of newspaper, keeping used oil patches in a tidy pile.

Gaetano, for the life of him, could not do anything, it

seemed, without leaving a mess. Patches and parts were all over his half of the table as he scrubbed the barrel of his CZ nine-millimeter.

The success of their strike depended on taking out the CID agents first. If they failed, the whole mission would be a waste.

Cotrone would take out the men in the van. The MP-7's 4.6x30mm cartridge was small like a handgun round but packed the potency of a rifle. The round was more than able to pierce the van's metal and continue through any living bodies inside.

Levasseur and Gaetano had the house. Levasseur hoped Gaetano was a much more disciplined fighter than he was at pretty much any other activity.

Two a.m. Street lamps burned brightly. Scattered porch lights illuminated homes. Every now and then a motion-sensor light blared briefly before snapping off. A cool wind blew but Cotrone felt nothing but a flush of heat throughout his entire body.

The MP-7 was slung under his right arm, partially concealed by a coat dangling past his waist.

He approached the van. Sweat beaded on his forehead and trickled behind his left ear. He was breathing too fast for somebody out for a walk and what the hell was he doing out this late anyway?

Nobody sat in front of the van. Duh. They'd be in back watching the Walkers on equipment similar to what they had inside the house.

Twenty yards. No alarm so far.

Levasseur and Gaetano would not cross the street until the van was secured, and Cotrone's throat suddenly dried up. He wasn't usually an assassin. He'd only ever killed three people, two in self-defense and this kind of attack was foreign to him. He was the surveillance guy. The getaway driver. Once the CID agents in the van were dead, his next task was to keep the car running for when the other two completed their part of the assignment.

The original plan had only called for him to drive.

He liked the original plan better. But then Graypoole had to change the plan.

Steps away now. Something inside the van shifted and banged against the wall.

Now! Cotrone whipped up the HK, his thumb clicking off the safety as his index finger slipped over the trigger. A silencer slightly extended the length of the weapon.

The MP-7 rocked against his shoulder and the loud and rapid thumping of the silenced shots sounded like heavy books dropping flat on a desk. Cotrone emptied the magazine into the side of the van, hearing screams as the slugs found their marks. The sub gun clicked empty. Cotrone changed mags and went to the rear, blasted the locks with a short burst and flung open one of the back doors. Both CID men were down in a puddle of blood mixed with broken pieces of electronic equipment. The puddle became a pool as Cotrone stood there.

Cotrone sprinted back to the house, lungs burning, nearly hyperventilating. As he approached the house, he saw Levasseur and Gaetano run across the street to the Walker house.

Levasseur and Gaetano crossed the driveway to the side of the house where Walker kept his garbage cans. The cans sat in front of a gate near the water meter. He couldn't have made it easier, Levasseur thought, as he and Gaetano stepped onto the meter, then onto the cans and then braced a hand atop the gate to swing over. They landed hard, bending knees to absorb the impact. A motion light flashed on. Good news and bad news. Bad because the CID man inside knew where they were. Good because the light lit the side passage and Walker was organized enough to have properly lined his yard gear against the fence. No debris impeded their progress.

They ran to the back yard, guns up, hearing shouts of alarm inside.

The killers rounded the back patio. Gaetano scooped up a metal chair with his free hand and flung it through the glass patio doors. The crash of glass seemed to shake the ground. His stock went up a little in Levasseur's book.

Gaetano went in first, Levaaseur ducking to avoid the pointy edges still in the door frame.

Pistol fire cracked and Levasseur felt a bullet hiss past his head.

"What was that?" Penny Walker said, sitting up in bed.

"Get the girls and lock yourselves in this room," Walker said as he rolled off the bed and collected a shotgun from the closet.

"Honey?"

"Don't forget the revolver in the dresser," he said, and went out of the room.

He found the CID man, a sergeant named Finnegan, in the hallway. His daughters rushed down toward him, nightgowns flapping, talking hurriedly, gasping when they saw the shotgun and Walker pushed them toward the master bedroom.

"I can't raise the van," the sergeant said.

"Follow me," Walker said, taking the lead and keeping low with the shotgun in both hands, a standard police Remington 870. Loaded with double-o buckshot, a blast could bring down any two-legged threat.

CHAPTER 24

—◆—

Even with the darkness in the hall, Walker moved with ease. His leg didn't bother him.

They rounded the corner to the kitchen as the patio door shattered inward. The metal chair landed on the tile with a loud clang.

"Down, General!"

Walker hit the floor, the shotgun tucked tight into his shoulder. Finnegan fired twice as two figures entered, both rounds missing. Walker fired. The muzzle blast lit the room for a split second and the buckshot connected with the lead intruder, tearing into his flesh with a wet slap. The intruder dropped and slid across the floor, banging against the metal chair.

Finnegan hopped over the general as Walker pumped the 870's action. The second intruder dodged left, deeper into the kitchen. Walker jumped up. A string of shots cracked and Walker collided with Finnegan's body as the sergeant fell.

Walker fell over, too, Finnegan landing on top of him, the dead man's weight pinning Walker's left side. He fired a blast for effect, heard glass and cabinetry shatter, and rolled away with a grunt. He bumped a table leg. As he pumped another shell, the second intruder fired twice. Walker screamed as the slugs struck. One in the shoulder, the other near his neck. Walker tasted blood on his lip.

He stifled another cry and lay still, pulse pounding in his head. The beam of a flashlight shined around him and blinked out. No use firing where the light was. Walker heard the intruder's shuffling footsteps as he changed positions.

Walker rolled onto his damaged left arm, grunting as he dragged himself across the tile. At least he slid easily. He reached the carpet of the adjoining dining room but then the doorway splintered as a shot cracked. Footsteps pounded. Walker raised the 870 with one hand. He fired. The strobe effect of the muzzle blast revealed the intruder rushing toward him but also revealed a miss. And Walker couldn't move his other arm to cycle the action. He let out a yell of defiance and pain.

The kitchen light snapped on. Walker recoiled from the sudden brightness, but not before he saw Penny with the revolver standing and aiming like he'd taught her, a classic isosceles stance. Legs spread, gun in both hands with the arms making a triangle. It might not be "special forces approved" but the general knew it served a functional purpose.

The intruder was caught in the open, a gun behind him and Walker straight ahead. Walker locked eyes with the man, who raised his pistol and then the magnum in Penny's hand thundered once, twice, a third time.

The last thing Walker heard before he passed out was his wife, screaming.

There's always one thing you can't count on, Levasseur decided. In this case, two. Walker knew how to fight, hence their original ambush plan. His wife knew some things, too. They should have checked her out more thoroughly than they had, but now it was too late. He raised his gun to put Walker down. If wifey hesitated a little, he could get her too.

But then the hammer struck. A hard blow against his right side. The bullet burned through his torso. He started to fall by the time the second round struck and Levasseur landed on hands and knees. He was finished. And then the third bullet smacked into his body and all feeling evaporated and the lights went out.

Dane, McConn and Stone loaded their gear into the jet's cargo hold in the rear of the plane. They stayed hunched under the plane, the rear wings and engines above. When Stone pushed the cargo door closed and turned the latch, Dane straightened, only to bash his head on the fuselage. He cursed.

"Planes weren't built for tall guys, Steve," Stone said.

Dane stifled further retort with a grimace, his right hand pressed hard on top of his head.

Nina and Hana, already aboard with a bottle of vodka between them and half-full glasses, were snickering at their own joke as the men boarded. They had started early, Dane noticed when he collected both from their hotel room, but at least the mood was a little lighter. Hana's father made it through the night, and the doctors said his prognosis looked good. When she heard the news, relief washed over Hana's face like a wave. Dane didn't begrudge her needing a few drinks after the ordeal.

Stone stepped into the cockpit to confer with the pilot. Dane and McConn found seats and strapped in.

"You two getting along?" Dane said.

"Fabulously," Nina said. "We have a lot in common. She went to boarding school, and I didn't."

The two women laughed.

Dane shook his head. "Gonna be a long flight."

"Oh, have a drink, honey." Nina snatched the bottle. "But get your own, these vitamins are for us girls."

Hana said nothing but regarded Dane with glassy eyes.

Stone joined them and found his seat. "Weather clear all the way to Zurich," he said.

The engines spooled up, their rumble muted, but Dane let out a satisfied sigh. They were on their way once again.

Presently the jet soared to 25,000 feet and leveled off.

Dane took off his seatbelt and reclined his seat.

"I don't see anybody following us," Dane reported from the back seat. He leaned against the backrest, knees on the seat. Stone drove. They'd rented a larger Mercedes SUV after clearing customs at Zurich Airport.

Nina, also watching, agreed. "Either they're being careful, or we got here before they did."

"I'm surprised you can see straight."

"I only drank *half* the bottle, dear."

Dane finally sat forward, buckled up and Nina did likewise. They occupied the third rear seat in the SUV. McConn sat in the middle, alone; Stone and Hana sat up front.

"Where to, Hana?" Dane said.

"Barclays," she said. "Beethovenstrasse 19."

"Isn't that our bank?" Nina said.

"Yes. They know us there, Hana, we won't have any trouble."

"What about after?" McConn said.

"Don't jinx it, cowboy," Dane said.

It was a nice drive at least, even with traffic. Zurich wasn't one of Dane's favorite cities, but he still enjoyed visiting. The snow-capped Alps stood in the distance, a sharp contrast to the antiseptic architecture of the city. The Alps oozed life and stirred emotion; the city felt like a museum with Do Not Touch signs every five meters.

The Alps held a special place in Dane's heart, but not for a reason any "normal" person might identify with. They looked serene but the territory was formidable and he'd once left two bodies somewhere in those jagged peaks. The incident happened during one of his first missions for the Agency, where he went into the mountains looking for a cache of gold coins allegedly hidden by al-Qaeda operatives. Dane wasn't the only one looking for the gold, as a team from AQ and two fortune hunters were also after the loot. Dane beat al-Qaeda to the stash, but the fortune hunters met him there. The fire fight didn't last long. Dane put the men down. He took out two men with automatic weapons while armed only with a pistol. He'd overcome terrible odds. He'd won. The following rush made him feel invincible. Shortly after, he almost died in the helicopter crash and never felt invincible again. Those back-to-back events showed him he needed to take advantage of all that life had to offer. Life was an adventure to be *lived* and ultimately meant breaking away from Agency employment and taking on the unknown challenges that never failed to show him how sweet life could be when you faced it head-on and served as a reminder he had a responsibility to be the champion others lacked. He welcomed the responsibility, at least until a bullet stopped him. Someday, somewhere, he'd be called to account.

But not today.

"Wow, look," Nina said. They were driving over a bridge, the Limmat River below. The river intersected the city and the wide waterway accommodated craft of all configurations. Nina pointed to an enclosed yacht, quite large, complete with blacked-out windows and a roof-mounted radar dish.

"We're not buying a yacht, either," Dane said.

Stone cleared the bridge and continued on, jumping on an expressway for two exits. Another couple of turns. But Dane knew they were still a few miles away.

"You see something, Dev?" Dane said. He unbuckled his seatbelt to look out the back window.

"Just making sure," Stone replied. "There was a taxi sticking to us pretty good."

Stone turned up Beethovenstrasse and the tall steel-and-glass Barclays building towered above all other structures on the street like a behemoth. Godzilla ready to pounce.

The parking garage across the street displayed a sign saying spaces remained, so Stone pulled in and found an empty slot in a back corner. The rest of the level was crammed with vehicles.

Dane exited the SUV with Hana. He told Stone to stay with the vehicle and directed Nina and McConn to scout for potential trouble.

Dane and Hana crossed the street, squinting against the sun's glare off the glass of the huge bank building.

The lobby was polished mirror-bright. Spotless floor,

walls bare but for a minimum of decoration. Teller windows lined the wall in front of them, each teller busy with a customer and a line fifteen deep. Dane led Hana to an area with six desks neatly lined three-by-three. Only one was currently occupied. The sign on the man's desk said Special Accounts.

The man looked up from a chart as Dane approached.

"Ah, hello, Herr Dane." He rose and extended a hand. Dane shook it with a smile.

"Peter, this is Hana Kader, she has a safe deposit box we need to access. Hana, Peter Bergstrom. Best banker in Zurich."

The man actually blushed a little as he denied the allegation. He wore a suit more expensive than anything in Dane's wardrobe. His round pot belly confirmed his middle age, but his hair was black as night.

"What is your account number, Fraulein?" He passed her a blank sheet of paper and a pen. Hana wrote out the ten-digit number. Bergstrom typed it into the computer, made a note of his own and asked Dane and Hana to follow him.

They went through a door marked Private and descended stairs to a maze of safe deposit boxes. Bergstrom led them down a row, turned left and stopped midway down the next row. He inserted a key in a box marked 047. Hana inserted her own key in the second lock and they turned at the same time.

"Return the key to me when you're done," Bergstrom said. "Time for a cigar later, Herr Dane?"

"This is a quick trip, Peter, sorry."

"Next time." Bergstrom departed with a smile. Dane and Hana waited until the banker was long gone.

She opened the door of the box and removed a rectangular case, flat black with no markings. Lifting the lid, she revealed the thumb drive inside.

"There it is. Everything my father collected on Graypoole."

Dane picked up the memory stick and dropped it in the inside pocket of his jacket.

"Let's—"

The overhead lights began flashing on and off. Hana gasped. The shrill tone of a fire alarm pierced through the ceiling.

Dane dialed Nina. "Somebody's pulled the fire alarm, get ready."

"Copy."

Dane stowed his cell as Bergstrom hurriedly rounded the corner. "Fire alarm, Herr Dane, we must clear the building!"

CHAPTER 25

—■—

Graypoole's team in Zurich, led by one Michel Badeaux, closed in on the bank.

Badeaux, in a separate car from the SUV his men occupied, parked on the street. Through their interconnected earpieces, Badeaux's crew said they were in the garage and weren't far from Dane's Mercedes.

"Only one man in the vehicle," the crew chief said.

Badeaux, wearing aviators with a tan top-coat over a gray suit, stood outside Barclays watching the street. "Where are the others?"

"Must have exited before we got here."

"I'm going inside. Wait for my signal."

"Which will be?"

"The fire alarm, what else?"

Badeaux put his hands in the top-coat pockets as he headed for the front doors, the bright reflection off the glass unable to penetrate the aviators' tint. He removed the sunglasses when he stepped into the lobby.

So if he were a fire alarm, where would he hide? Badeaux chuckled to himself. His right hand remained in the top-coat pocket and he flicked off the safety of the automatic hidden there. The gun was not his preferred Glock-18, which he'd left behind in Paris, but an untested nine-millimeter FN FNX. Sure, he had 17-rounds in the magazine, but no idea if the gun fired straight. There'd been no time to practice. He cursed his circumstances. Sometimes you had to improvise with what tools you had available.

He spotted the fire alarm. The red box with the pull-down switch was on the bare wall near the desks. Badeaux took two steps toward it and stopped. Across the floor, a door marked Private swung open and a paunchy gent came through, not even giving Badeaux a glance as he crossed to the teller cage to speak with a woman behind one of the windows.

Badeaux reached the alarm, pulled the lever, and dropped behind the desk a foot away. As the alarm blared, he took out the FN pistol and curled his finger around the trigger.

The paunchy man moved fast as everybody made for the exit. The man dashed through the Private door once again.

Bergstrom led the way back up the steps with Dane and Hana behind him, Dane clutching his gun close to his leg.

The alarm could only mean one thing.

As they reached the door, Dane said, "Stop," and cut in front of Bergstrom, popping the door open an inch.

"Herr Dane, what—"

Dane held up a hand and peeked out.

The two bank guards were ushering out the last of the customers and staff. The shrill alarm was louder now. One guard spotted Dane and urgently waved him forward.

"Stay behind me," Dane ordered. He moved through the doorway first, the other two behind him. The teller cage was empty, the loan desks deserted; there was not a soul other than the guards, yet the ghosts of battles past whispered all was not well.

Dane moved faster, Hana and Bergstrom shuffling to keep up and then a gunman in a top-coat rose from behind a desk.

Dane stepped in front of Hana. She collided with a yelp and fell, jostling Dane's aim in the process. The gunman fired once. Somebody screamed. Dane fired once. The gunman's head snapped back, painting the wall behind with a splash of red.

Dane yelled for the guards but they were already running with their own revolvers in hand.

Hana, still sprawled on the floor, was unhurt, but Bergstrom had fallen next to her and continued to wail. His white shirt was stained red, the gunman's bullet having punched solidly through his shoulder.

Dane put away his .45 and helped the guards get the best banker in Zurich to his feet. The guards carried him out while Dane took Hana's hand and broke right. Behind the loan desks was an emergency exit. As they crashed through the door into an alley and made for the street in front of the bank, the first fire engine pulled up, sirens loud. Traffic behind the engine stopped while everybody after the engine kept going and soon the street was nearly clear of vehicles. Plenty of pedestrians remained to watch the action.

Dane hauled Hana across the street. Nina met them at the sidewalk, her face full of concern. The three hustled for the garage. McConn caught up, staying behind Hana, and the sounds in front of the bank faded as they entered the parking structure.

"What happened?" Nina said as they hurried past the

parked cars for the Mercedes a few yards away.

"One gunman. I took him out but—"

McConn shouted, "Get down!"

Three shooters emerged from between cars across the aisle, each toting stubby CZ Scorpion Eon3 submachine guns.

Dane grabbed Hana by the shoulders and forced her between a truck and a van, the young woman letting out a shriek as Dane landed on top of her and Nina and McConn opened fire. The popping of their handguns was soon drowned out by the crackle of the Scorpions.

The truck and van rocked as bullets tore through metal, glass shattering, shards raining down on Dane. He felt a few cut his neck and sink down the back of his shirt. He cursed as Hana screamed again, the Scorpions going silent as Nina's nine-millimeter cracked twice more.

"Gotta move," McConn shouted, leaping over Dane and Hana to the aisle ahead.

Dane and Hana jumped up, Nina shoving Dane forward as they gained the next aisle and ran, keeping low.

"I got one," Nina said, "but there's two left."

More Scorpion fire smashed into the cars blocking them from the gunners, Nina and McConn stretching out their right arms to fire blindly as they ran.

The Mercedes SUV screeched to a stop ahead of them, Stone shooting out the window. The Scorpions stopped for a moment. Dane and the others piled in and the shooters opened up again as Stone burned rubber for the exit. A stray round nicked the rear window. Stone reached the street and wrenched the wheel to the right, speeding down the empty road with the fire engine behind him, pedestrians agape and police cruisers approaching in the distance.

CHAPTER 26

━━━━━●━━━━━

Stone made the first right, the SUV's tires screaming again.

Dane fidgeted in his seat, then removed his jacket and pulled up his shirt. The pieces of glass dropped onto the seat. Only one was a little red and a bloody spot quickly appeared on the back of his shirt.

"Anybody got any holes in them?" Stone said.

Hana sat slumped in her seat, staring straight ahead. She was wedged between Dane and Nina and Nina put an arm around her.

"None that we weren't born with, right, kid?" Nina said.

Hana concurred.

"Straight to the airport, Dev, we gotta fly."

"They got General Walker," Lukavina said.

"Oh, no." Dane said into his cell phone, standing against the galley counter at back of Stone's jet. They were still on the airport tarmac.

"He'll live," Lukavina said, "but he was shot twice. We were trying to protect him from the threat only to have that very threat living across the street from his house."

"I'm sorry, Len."

"Sometimes we can't win."

"Maybe you'll like my news about Zurich. Stone is setting up the computer now so we can look at Kader's files. I'll get back with you when we have something."

"No, you'll send the information to me."

"Of course, Len, after we pick out the juiciest lead."

"Are you done fooling around?"

"You weren't in San Francisco."

"Wherever you go next, drop Hana off at the nearest US Embassy. We'll pick her up. We're moving her father into protective custody as well, until this is over."

Dane said okay, hung up and joined the others.

Stone was at the table, busy with the laptop connected to the TV. The forward big screen was blank. "Almost got it," he said.

Dane stood with hands on hips. Hana sat across from Nina, having barely touched her drink. She held the glass but had a stare fixed on the carpet. He went over and sat beside her.

"You okay?"

"I need to talk to my father," Hana said.

Dane nodded and took out his phone. He called Kader direct, the line answered by one of his men.

"It's Dane, Hana wants to talk."

He handed Hana the phone and joined Stone at the table. He had the files on the thumb drive displayed on the monitor. "What do we have?"

Nina and McConn wandered over too.

Stone scrolled through pages of typed notes. "A lot. Kader basically kept a diary, making notes with corresponding dates and crossing out what wasn't actionable any longer. But see these notations here, here? This is all stuff the CIA used to assassinate the elder Graypoole and go after his lieutenants."

"Anything not notated that way?" Nina said.

Dane said, "Go to the end. We don't want the old info. It's useless by now."

Stone jumped to the end of the file, finding more notes. "Here's a recent entry." He scrolled up and stopped when the screen filled with a photo of an older man.

"Mister Donovan Black. American father, French mother, lives in France on an estate. He inherited the place fifteen years ago from his maternal grandfather."

"He's a retired investor," Dane said.

"How do you know?"

Nina said, "Because we worked for him once."

"What kind of job?" Stone said.

"He wanted an armed escort for some expensive paintings. We moved them from one place to another."

"Are you sure it was art?" McConn said.

"Never had a reason to check more than once," Dane said. "He collects art. A lot of it."

McConn continued, "Broke a hip six months ago so he walks with a slight limp and uses a cane, but he's in decent shape for a man pushing 80."

"Any hint he finances terrorists?" Dane said.

"None that I can find and there's a note here that says why the CIA didn't act on this information when Kader presented it. Could be they never made a connection. His official money trail is clean, but he does fund a charity that could be funky. Lots of redirects, but the Agency could never find definitive evidence, according to Kader. He argued otherwise but admits he found no hard proof. If he is funding Graypoole, the charity is where to look."

"What does the charity do?"

"Supports art education in Europe. Every year he hosts an auction at his estate and the proceeds go to the charity."

Nina said, "When's the next auction?"

Stone highlighted a series of dates, many that had come and gone over the last few years, but only the most recent entry wasn't crossed out. "Three days from now. Tickets are sold out but they'll let last-minute people in for a five-thousand-dollar donation."

"Let's do it," Dane said.

Black's estate sat outside Guerande northeast of Pornichet. Dane and Nina, in a rented BMW, followed Route de Herbignae all the way to Kerguence Road. A short hook around a lake and the gate of Black's property loomed ahead.

It was a very nice ride with little traffic and the lush countryside along Route de Herbignae made the ride even more pleasant. It was easy to forget why they were there, but Dane didn't let that happen. Lilly Klove's face was never far from his mind's eye.

The five cars ahead passed through the gate one-by-one and then it was Dane's turn to present his invitation to the guard. The guard wore a white shirt and black slacks with the name of his security company on one sleeve. No weapon. He spoke English, cleared Dane and Nina and told them to enjoy their stay. "Follow the other cars," he added.

Dane steered the BMW along the access road.

The main house covered most of the property, multiple stories; two similar buildings sat on either side. The trail of cars led to the building on the left of the main house, so the other was either servant's quarters or more guest space.

Valets met them at the front of the building. Porters unloaded the luggage. Dane and Nina's porter loaded their suitcases onto a cart and led them inside.

The entryway opened on a large room with marble tile and support beams. Paintings hung on walls. Dane recognized a few. A Rembrandt. Van Gogh. There was a lot of money on those walls. A short elevator ride brought them to the fourth floor. The porter deposited them at their room and Dane tipped the man well.

They started to unpack and made small talk about the trip. Dane extracted the Stone-supplied shaver and turned it on. He continued the small talk as he moved around the room. A light on the shaver remained green all around the room. He checked the bathroom and closet. The green light remained. Black's people had not placed any eavesdropping devices in the room.

Yet.

Dane turned off the shaver. "Clear."

Nina opened the curtains to let the sun inside. The view showed part of the countryside and the motorway they'd traveled on.

Dane joined her at the window. Two riders on horseback rode in the distance.

"It's like a regular five-star," she said.

Dane removed the Scoremaster from his case and loaded a magazine. "I'm thinking of what's beneath the surface." He put the gun in his shoulder holster.

"Come and sit down," she said. "Relax a bit."

Dane let out a grunt and took the chair beside her. He placed his arms on the armrests and stared ahead.

"What's the problem?"

"Did we do anything wrong when we transported Black's art?"

"If we did, he hid it well."

"I don't like being played."

"This auction covers three days," she said. "If we can't come up with answers in that time, we need another line of work."

"I'm bothered neither the CIA nor Kader found anything to hang on Black."

"The CIA and Kader aren't *us*," Nina said.

Dane grinned. "You always know how to spin it, baby," he said.

CHAPTER 27

———■———

Dane, wearing his black suit, white shirt, black tie, gave the cuff of his right sleeve a quick tug as he stood in line with Nina beside him. She wore a red mini-dress, strapless, with matching stilettos.

"A Russian wearing red, how original," Dane cracked.

"My underwear is white and blue," she said.

"In that order?"

She jabbed him in the belly.

"I'll find out later." He winked at her.

They waited in line to enter the reception hall where there would be drinks and appetizers prior to a four-course dinner.

They examined the faces around them, mostly couples but some lone stragglers as well. Nobody tripped their mental mug files, but the night was young.

Presently they filed into the wide reception room. Large open floor, domed ceiling, tall tables and stools lining the walls. The diamond chandeliers looked more expensive than Dane's entire Savile Row wardrobe. Waiters and waitresses wandered with trays of champagne but Dane and Nina headed for the bar instead. The bartender mixed a pair of martinis to their specifications. Regular dirty martini for Nina. Dane specified a vodka/gin mix with a splash of vermouth and a dash of water after the pour. The bartender raised an eyebrow. Dane explained the water leveled out the rubbing alcohol smell of the combined vodka and gin.

"You can drink it like water," Dane said as he accepted the glass. "Problem is, after three or four you suddenly remember it isn't water."

The bartender grinned and moved down the bar to help another customer.

"I'm bored," Nina said as they watched faces. She finished most of the martini and ate the olives.

"You're not the only one," Dane said. Most of his drink remained. He took another sip. "Look over there."

He gestured with the rim of his glass. Nina looked in the indicated direction.

A short woman with glasses and red hair, tied back in a ponytail, occupied a spot along the opposite wall. No companion. She wore a blue strapless dress with a V-neck.

"What is *she* doing here?" Nina said.

"Well *she* is with Interpol. *She* is probably here for the same reason we are."

"She tried to arrest us once, remember?"

"Admit it, we probably deserved it."

Rachael Satastini turned her head to examine the other side of the room. She raised her glass to Dane and Nina; Dane saluted back.

"Put your arm down before I snap it off at the elbow."

Dane laughed. He took a drink and set down the martini. He said, "Let's flip for who has to talk to her."

"I'll do it. After dinner."

"Fair enough."

She swallowed her martini in one throw. "I need another drink." Nina asked for a refill.

Dane glanced at the entryway as a gray-haired man with a cane entered. He held the cane in his right hand but didn't lean on it too heavily and he kept his back straight. Dane wasn't the only one to notice him. Right away guests came over to say hello, forcing Donovan Black to shake awkwardly with his left hand. He muttered, "Pardon my hip," to several well-wishers. Nobody seemed to mind. Faces lit up around him.

Dane drank his martini and watched the man work the room. Was he really connected with Graypoole? He didn't seem bad on the surface and even the best chameleons had a tell somewhere. Dane hadn't seen one when he worked for the man, and he didn't see one now.

Maybe Black was simply *very* good at concealing his true nature.

Most monsters were.

"Mr. Dane, what a pleasure! Ms. Talikova, you look stunning."

Dane and Nina exchanged pleasantries with Black. He'd made the rounds and saved them for last.

"When I saw your names on the guest list, I admit it was a surprise."

Black spoke with a very deep, soothing voice. The kind you want your doctor to use when he tells you your heart needs a new canooter valve.

"We're between jobs," Dane said, "and who doesn't like a good cause?"

"There are some wonderful paintings up for auction, including a few surprises not in the catalogue." Black grinned. "It's a tradition. Surprise finale, if you will."

Nina said, "What's for dinner?"

Black let out a bellow of a laugh. "Never change, Ms. Talikova. The world will be worse off if you do. We have a very good menu tonight, you won't be disappointed. Now please excuse me. I came in here to announce it's time for the first course."

Black stepped away, quieted the guests and made his announcement. He showed everyone into the dining hall, which resembled the reception room with long tables lined down the center of the floor. Everybody found a place setting. Dane noticed Rachael Satastini sat one table over.

What was she doing here?

He looked around some more.

"What?" Nina said.

"Black isn't here."

Nobody noticed Donovan Black slip away.

He stood by the doors of the dining room as his guests filed in, exchanging smiles and nods and wishing all a good meal. Then he left for his private elevator down a nearby hallway. He exited on the second floor and cursed the cane and his hip as he made for his office. He couldn't move like he used to. Age and injury. The bane of mankind, specifically a man like him. There was still so much he wanted to accomplish. He needed his body on board with his goals.

Black entered his office. A large fish tank covered one wall, the fish inside swimming lazily around castles and other structures.

Near Black's desk, in front of a computer and a set of monitors, sat a younger man with blonde hair, slicked back. He wore a dark suit.

"Any problems, Sean?" Black said as he made his way to the younger man.

Sean O'Malley shook his head. "Nobody here who wasn't invited, but two people did raise an alert."

O'Malley wound back footage on one of the monitors. A facial recognition program boxed each face; the computer showed the rapid change of pictures and ID information of each guest. O'Malley froze the process when Dane and Nina appeared on the monitor.

Black said, "Yes, I know them. They've worked for me in the past."

"Shall I check them out? They're known to work for the CIA."

"I know what they're doing here. I'd like to give them a length of rope to hang themselves with." Black made for his desk and sat down with a wince. He rubbed his right leg.

"Getting old is an awful thing, Sean."

"Yes, sir."

CHAPTER 28

———

Dinner did not disappoint, from the first course, a tomato soup, to dessert, a chocolate mousse, all delightful and Nina said so.

The reception hall re-opened once again with a jazz band playing on a small stage.

"Care to dance?" Dane said.

"Not in these shoes."

"You'll live, come on."

They cut the floor to an up-tempo number, dodging other couples in some cases, spinning around to see where their friend from Interpol was hiding.

"In the corner, talking to a Hispanic chap," Nina said. "And he's wearing white."

When the song ended, they headed for the bar. Fresh drinks in hand, they found another table. Some guests were heading for Black's auction display and his personal museum, so there was an ebb-and-flow to the number of guests drinking and dancing.

"Look at her body language," Dane said. "She isn't happy with her friend."

"Why are you looking at her body?"

"Not tonight, honey."

Nina let out a sigh. "I suppose this is one of those times where the sisterhood takes precedence over shoving her off a cliff," she said. "Pardon me while I do a bit of rescuing."

"Don't hit her till you know why she's here," Dane said.

"I *know* that."

"Just reminding you." He winked.

She glared and headed for Rachael Satastini, Interpol agent.

When Nina neared, the Hispanic in white was leaning close to Rachael, who put a hand out to halt him. As she started to speak, Nina jumped in.

"Is he bothering you, Rachael?"

"A little."

"Who is your friend?" said the man in white with a gleam in his eye.

"I don't know what name she's using tonight. What's your name tonight, lady in red?"

"My real name."

"Oh. Then this is Nina. Nina, meet Paco."

"How lovely to—*ahhhhhhhhhh!*"

As Paco reached for Nina's hand, presumably to kiss it, she grabbed his wrist and twisted, forcing the man to turn and arch his back.

"Leave us. Now."

"Sorry, Paco," the Interpol lady said, "she was raped in a porta potty once."

Nina let go and the man departed unsteadily, trying to straighten his outfit as he walked.

Nina put her hands on her hips. "That was really, really gross, *and* uncalled for."

"You'd have said it too."

"What are you doing here?"

"I should ask you." Rachael peeked around Nina. "Steve is looking hunky tonight."

"He goes home with *me*, tart."

Rachael laughed. Sipped her wine. "You never let me down. Sit. Come on, sit."

"I like standing."

"Suit yourself. I'm here on business."

"So are we."

"To steal something? All the paintings have electronic tabs so forget it. They're bugged, too. All the schleps going to ogle them are telling Black how much they'll pay without knowing it."

"All for a good cause."

Another sip of wine. "That's the rumor."

"So why does your agency care?"

"Why does the CIA care?"

Nina narrowed her eyes.

"This room might be wired."

"There's a reason I'm close to the stage."

Nina finally sat down.

"Good girl."

"Shut up." She leaned closer to Rachael. "We need to work together, not play antagonist."

"You still mad about Jamaica?"

"Yes."

"Then why should I bother?"

"I'm willing to forgive and forget."

"How Christian of you. Oh, wait, was that offensive?"

Nina kept her mouth shut and her eyes locked on the redhead's. Finally, Rachael Satastini sighed.

"Okay, truce. You're right. We can probably help each

other."

"You first."

"Interpol has been tracking a man named Derya Teke. Big gangster in Kabul. Sold a lot of guns to insurgents who killed a lot of coalition troops. Now he has somehow acquired a bomb and Black is writing a check."

"Why does Black—"

"No idea. We intercepted calls between Teke and Black and a person named Mr. X. Teke will bring the bomb here since Black has the smuggling route worked out. This is also where Teke collects his money."

"Who is Mr. X?"

"Who do you think?"

"Graypoole?"

"Graypoole is dead."

"His son isn't."

"How juicy."

"Where's Black's office?"

"Second floor, end of the hall. See that hallway over there? Private elevator. Or use the stairs at the front door. But be careful. Black's number two is a man named Sean O'Malley. He doesn't mess around."

"There isn't a man I can't handle," Nina said, slipping off the stool. "Keep your head down."

"Oh, I *will*," Rachael said. She winked. Nina shook her head and returned to Dane after a stop at the bar for another refill.

Later, the wait staff opened some side doors to let guests mingle on the outdoor patio. Dane and Nina migrated there. Dane lit a cigar and added to the accumulating tobacco smoke already in the air.

Nina provided a rundown on her chat with Rachael, using different words here and there in case of surveillance.

"Is Teke here?" Dane said.

"She didn't say. If he's not here now he'll slip in overnight."

Dane nodded. He puffed on the cigar. "Auction starts at three tomorrow."

She leaned close and nuzzled his neck. "We still have a few hours."

Dane shut the door to their room and turned the lock.

"Boy, sure was a nice dinner," Nina said, kicking off her heels. She left them on the floor and reached up her dress to peel off her stockings. She wrapped them in a ball and dropped them near her heels.

She continued the senseless dinner chatter as Dane went around the room with the bug sweeper. He paused at the lamp near the bed. The indicator on the shaver glowed red this time.

Nina smiled and took the sweeper from Dane's hand, and set it down on the nightstand. She stepped in front of him, reached back with both arms and pulled down the zipper on the back of her dress. Dane chuckled and pulled her to him.

She hadn't been lying about her underwear.

They gave the bug something to transmit the rest of the night.

CHAPTER 29

Derya Teke was a little thin but the designer suit fit perfectly, with a little extra breathing space between his neck and collar. He wore no beard and his hair was cut short, his cheek bones and jaw prominent, the only really interesting feature being his hooked nose. It was a normal nose until the tip, which bent at a slight angle. Teke wished he could say it was the result of an injury, but no such luck. He'd been born with it. He had enough money to have it surgically repaired, but the fear of a mistake causing the nose to look worse held him back.

He sat in the rear of the limo with his legs crossed, hands on lap, briefcase on the seat beside him. He stared out at the countryside without really seeing it. He had his mind on the job at hand.

He was attending the auction to collect a payment, deliver a bomb for Donovan Black to ship via his nefarious ways and add a painting to his growing collection. Teke, an Afghan, had flirted with al-Qaeda and as a free-lance terrorist-for-hire, but quickly left when he realized he liked money and high living more than jihad. When Graypoole the Elder had come calling, Teke found somebody of like mind and pledged his allegiance. Now that his son was in charge, Teke was happy to be back in his primary business.

From his base of operations in Goa, India, he used the bottom level of his home to display his many paintings, some of which had gone missing from famous museums many years ago and he had a spot picked out for whatever he received from Donovan Black. He had nothing specific in mind. The auction would reveal something that struck his interest. He'd be given whatever he asked for and nuts to the high bidder. If said bidder had a complaint, Black would deal with him. Teke would remain far away from the transaction, as if he were on the other side of the planet.

The car stopped at the main gate of the Black home, the guard performed his cursory check and the driver continued through.

McConn and Stone hunkered at a hide site about 100 yards from the house. They had found a gully allowing them to set up a small camp to watch the house from the top, where they both lay on their stomachs with binoculars as the new arrival passed through the gates. The soft grass was the only luxury their hiding spot afforded.

But the morning dew had yet to dry and their clothes were wet. The morning chill showed no mercy in its bite.

"That one is late," Stone said.

"Another fat cat who gets to dine on caviar and stay warm while we're sleeping in the dirt," McConn said.

They had a pair of sleeping bags. Couldn't light a fire at night. Luckily the binoculars had night vision capability and allowed them to continue working well into the night until they absolutely had to sleep. The thermal sleeping

bags retained a lot of heat, but, to McConn, not enough. And then they only had cold MREs to eat. Probably the worst insult.

Furthermore, McConn had already gone twenty-four hours without hot coffee.

"I'd like to know why he's so tardy."

"Probably couldn't figure out which Rolex to bring, so he packed them all."

"Todd."

"What?"

"You're being annoying."

Donovan Black, in a blue suit and tie, entered his office, leaning on his cane as he stopped in front of Sean O'Malley and the surveillance gear.

"Anything?"

"Dane and Talikova have odd ideas about sex."

"That's not what I mean."

O'Malley consulted a sheet of paper. "Some of the guests talked money." He handed the sheet to his boss, who awkwardly folded it with one hand and placed it in the left side pocket of his suit pants.

"What else?"

"Teke is here. He's been shown into the dining room."

"Very good."

Black departed and made his way down the long hallway to the dining room. The walls were taller than average, decorated with either paintings of tapestries, another artistic design on the ceiling, which nobody ever really noticed. The wood flooring and walls were polished to a high sheen and Black found Teke examining the paintings with admiration. He moved from one to another and let out

an audible gasp. The gasp echoed a little.

"I'm surprised," Black said, "you didn't notice this piece sooner."

"You have the Marc Angelo. *The* Marc Angelo." Excitement grew in Teke's voice. "It's been missing for—"

"Over seventy years."

Black stopped beside Teke and looked up at the painting, which showed a man in black staring out an open window, a blank wall behind him, bright light shining through the window and leaving a spot on the floor. The man was reportedly the artist himself, the only known self-portrait of Marc Angelo.

"The Nazis were supposed to have destroyed the whole collection when they burned down—"

"This painting survived. The frame covers scarring along the edges."

"What would you take for it?"

"You can't sell what officially doesn't exist," Black said.

"Care to bet?" Teke said. He grinned. He finally offered Black a hand and they shook.

"Welcome, Derya. Please, sit."

They took seats at the table, Black hooking his cane on the edge of the table, where the tip dangled a little off the floor. He lifted a bell, shook it once and one of his servants appeared through a doorway. The servant held the door while another pushed a loaded cart into the room. Both servants began distributing hot plates, mugs and glasses in front of Black and his guest.

"I had the kitchen prepare an omelet based on my own recipe," Black said. "Meat, vegetables, extra peppers. At my age I've found my tongue doesn't taste as well as it used to." His voice took a grim tone as he added:

"Among other things. Anyway the extra spice provides a nice flavor."

Teke offered a half-smile in reply as he stirred creamer into his coffee.

The table set, the servants departed.

The omelet filled most of the plate, what little extra space there was occupied by diced and fried potatoes.

Black and Teke started eating.

"The bomb is in the trunk of my car," Teke said.

"How is it packed?"

"In a suitcase. It's heavy but one man can lift it. My driver is standing guard."

"We'll move it into the warehouse shortly."

"I can't wait for the auction."

"Pick whatever you want. Your payment will be included in the crate when we ship the painting to your home."

"You've scouted the route?"

Black nodded and swallowed. "I have a team spread out along the way. They'll intercept you at designated points and see you through to the next. Everything is secure. They report clear sailing all the way to Seattle."

"This is a delicious omelet," Teke said. "And you've thought of everything."

"Almost everything."

"What does that mean?"

"Operations like this always have problems, as you well know. Right now, I'm trying to sort out two in particular I hope to have resolved before you leave."

CHAPTER 30

◼━◼

The auction room filled promptly at three in the afternoon, after Black's guests had gone through a delicious breakfast, free time and lunch. The chairs were laid out in three sections, each seat facing a stage and podium. A velvet curtain edged the stage but did not cover up the totem-pole style wood carvings that stood on either side. The carvings appeared to be a trio of griffons sitting atop one another. The griffon on the bottom wore a grimace. He was less happy than his companions.

The room had bare walls and wood trim, white-coated servants lining the back wall. One had to only raise a hand to summon a servant who would procure any kind of requested beverage.

Dane and Nina sat in the middle row of the center section, directly in front of the stage. Nina placed her purse on the seat to her left and said to several inquiring guests it was already taken.

"I can't believe you made a deal with her," Dane said.

"You told me to get along."

"Maybe I'm a little mad about Jamaica still, too."

"You said we deserved it."

"That doesn't mean—here she is."

"I felt my ears burning," said Rachel Satastini. She dropped into the open seat. She and Nina sized each other up. Both wore tight party dresses of different colors; Dane had to admit they both looked good. Rachael's ended further above the knee than Nina's. Nina wore her hair tied back while Rachael's hung down her back.

"Hello, Steve," the Interpol woman said. "Long time."

"Should have been longer."

To Nina, she said: "Didn't you tell him of our arrangement?"

"I might have forgotten."

More guests filed in, Dane watching them find seats. Not all off the faces were familiar from last night, but still none jumped out as particular familiar.

"Over there, front row, left section," Rachael said.

Dane and Nina looked. A thin man with a hooked nose, in a sharp suit, sat with his hands folded and legs crossed. He spoke to nobody and ignored the other guests. The griffons seemed to occupy his attention than any of the activity around him.

"Derya Teke," Rachael said. "Our man with the bomb."

"He makes them himself?" Dane said.

"He only sells. Has himself a nice organization of people who make the stuff."

"Why is he here? Why not deliver and go?" Dane said.

"He wants a painting. Has a huge collection of his own."

Dane thought of the job he and Nina worked for Black. The crates could have been legit. Seeing the Teke connection in the flesh gave Dane had a strong suspicion he had been used. What had been in those crates and who had been hurt because of them? Or had the crate hidden illicit payments to others? He took a deep breath to calm his rising anger. He would have a few words with Black about the matter soon enough.

Somebody delivering a bomb to Black more or less confirmed he was a black hat, but was the bomb meant for Mason Graypoole? One of his field operatives?

Too many questions. Not enough time to find the answers.

Donovan Black stepped behind the podium, and lifted his free hand to the audience, who applauded politely. He gave a welcome speech, explained a little about his charity and how much had been given to art education after last year's auction, which elicited more applause and some whistles. Black hoped they could do the same this year, plus one dollar, because children deserve to have exposure to the world's great works of art. *A regular Jerry Lewis, this guy,* Dane thought.

Black introduced the auctioneer, a man with white hair who wore a tux too tight to contain his girth. The man took the podium while Black made his way to his seat in the front row of the middle section. He did not sit near Teke and they did not acknowledge each other.

The auctioneer and his two lovely assistants brought each item up for review and bidding. Every painting had a sheet draped over it, which one of the assistants removed with flourish upon announcement of the work. With each reveal some members of the audience consulted those beside them, whispers of interest filling the room. The auctioneer held up his gavel and announced each opening bid, and Dane, arms folded and legs crossed, kept an eye on Teke. The man showed no response to most of the offerings well into the first ninety minutes.

Dane wondered what he was waiting for and borrowed the catalogue from Nina to see if he could figure out what the man wanted.

The ladies on stage rolled out the next painting. A red sheet covered the front, and a growing anticipation filled the room as the auctioneer announced the lot number and the name of the painting.

"Lot Number Ten, a one-of-a-kind, Sergio Monte's *Born of Fire.*"

The two women yanked the drape away from the painting and some of the guests applauded.

It was a simple yet striking painting. Black background. Orange fire on the bottom half seemed to come alive as the light struck. Out of the flames, the upper torso of a not-quite-full-formed body, arms outstretched, head tilted back, mouth open. The color around the body matched the flames and also gave the illusion of emerging from the canvas.

"We open the bidding at $200,000 American. Do I have $200,000?"

Within three minutes the bidding had reached $350,000 with no end in sight. Derya Teke kept pushing it higher with a slight wave of his hand.

$400,000. And higher.

Presently one million and a hush fell over the audience. Monte's painting had a very short history, but it, like his other work, had taken the art world by storm and everybody wanted a piece of his work in their collection.

"The bidding stands at one-point-three-million American," the auctioneer said. "Do I have one-point-five? One-point-five million?"

Teke raised his hand.

"Do I have one-point-eight? One-point-eight million?"

Whispers. No takers.

"Going once. Twice. Sold for one-point-five million dollars."

Mild applause filled the hall as the woman on stage wheeled the painting out of sight.

Derya Teke had a wide smile on his face.

"He's not going to spend a dime," Dane said.

"What do you mean?"

"The painting is a bonus on top of whatever Black is giving him."

Dane couldn't see Black's reaction. The man remained up front, seemingly uninterested in the winning bidder's identity.

Rachael said, "They'll move that painting to the warehouse in the back of the estate."

"We'll check it out tonight," Dane said.

CHAPTER 31

—■———■—

Dane slipped out of the guest house on the pretense of needing fresh air, but no guards interfered with him and he wasn't alone. Several guests milled about the front courtyard, their voices carrying with the night, talk of the auction and other activities the main topic.

Dane's shoes crunched on the ground as he circled the back of the house, passing the servant's quarters and found the warehouse where Rachael Satastini said it would be. It sat about twenty yards from the main house. The construction matched the rest of the buildings, but the wide doors on one side and the bright lights and activity inside communicated its difference. Semi-trucks were backed against loading docks. A panel van sat to one side of the warehouse, the driver behind the wheel smoking a cigarette. Judging by the pile of butts outside his door, he'd been smoking a lot of them for a long time.

Dane, dressed in black, kept to the shadows behind the main house as he sought a darkened corner of the warehouse to use for his approach. The .45 rode behind his back, slightly longer because of the stubby silencer fitted on the end of the barrel.

The light inside cast odd shadows along the ground punctuated by streaks of illumination. Not the best for his purposes, but certainly nothing to which Dane couldn't adapt.

And then he opted for the obvious. He was a guest out for a walk. Why would there be anything nefarious going on at the warehouse?

He left the shadows and crossed the gap to the warehouse. No guards on this side. The shouts and commands from inside became clearer with each step. A crew was loading the trucks with the purchased paintings. Forklifts grumbled and the truck trailers shook as the work carried on.

Dane reached a corner and watched the line of semis. The busy crew seemed normal enough. What other cargo were they loading on those trucks?

Following the wall, Dane rounded a corner and stopped. He was at the opposite end where there were no lights. Cigarette butts littered the ground. Smoking area. He found a door and tested the knob. Unlocked. Dane pulled open the door and it squeaked on rusty hinges, but the noise inside more than covered up the sound.

Ahead was an open concrete-floor, most of the space occupied by sealed crates. As the forklift crews loaded each crate in turn, a foreman with a clipboard inspected the labels on the crates, comparing the labels with notes on his clipboard.

Across the floor, in a small kitchen area, five gunmen stood around with their weapons slung. Security, obviously, for the millions and millions of dollars of art in those crates. And a big problem for Dane.

He slipped through the doorway. In front of him,

against a wall, was a set of steps leading to the next level. Dane moved under the stairs, put his back to the wall. The foreman and a man with long hair man approached, heading for the stairs. Dane pressed back further into the staircase's shadow. The two men passed in front of the steps and entered an office around the corner. The foreman said, "Tell that future cancer patient in the van to move around to the back and we'll load the bomb. I'll tell Mr. Black and his guest."

The long-haired man departed. Dane heard a chair creak. Papers shuffled.

The door was steps away, but would the foreman hear? Dane had to chance it. He had the opportunity to hijack the bomb and get it away from here.

As he started to move, the phone in the office rang, and soon the foreman's attention was occupied with the call. Dane opened the door as far as he needed and slipped back into the night. He moved left. Around the corner, the driver of the panel van was reversing into position, the rear facing the wall. The long-haired man kept waving him closer until he shouted, "Stop!" The driver put the van in park. Exiting, he came around to open the rear doors. The long-haired man opened another door on that side of the warehouse and shouted, "Bring the box over here!"

Dane took out the suppressed .45 and clicked off the safety. A forklift with a thin man behind the wheel steered an unmarked crate into the back of the panel van. Once he backed out, the van's driver slammed the doors. Dane turned the corner and walked toward the van with both hands behind his back and the .45 in his right. His shoes crunched on something and the long-haired man snapped his head around.

"Who are you?" The long-haired man stepped forward.

The van driver pulled a gun.

"Whoa!" Dane said. "I'm out for a walk. Not trying to rip off anything."

"This is a restricted area, go back to your room."

Dane brought up the .45 and fired once. The long-haired man's head snapped back, parts of his brain splattering on the van. The driver let out half a scream before most of his head splattered on the van. Dane ran to the driver's side and jumped behind the wheel. He almost choked. The cabin reeked of cigarette smoke. The engine rumbled to life and Dane shoved the gear into Drive. He started forward, making a sharp left, and started putting distance between the van and the building.

Automatic weapons fire strafed the side of the van, popping through the metal behind Dane, tearing into the passenger seat. Dane gave it more gas but then a loud boom filled the cabin. The rear end sank. The engine revved but the van wouldn't move.

Dane hopped out, the .45 up in both hands. The gunmen he'd counted in the kitchen charged his way, two stopping to align their sights. Dane shot one, then dodged to the front of the van as the other fired. The bullets kicked up geysers of dirt where Dane had been, some of it landing on the hood as Dane braced his arm on the fender.

More shots riddled the van as the gunmen spread out. Dane fired once around the driver's side, then rushed over to the passenger side to catch another gunman closing in. Dane shot him in the chest. As he hustled back to the opposite side again, suddenly two of the shooters were on top of him, their gun butts hammering into his body. Dane went down and tried to get up but the struggle ended when one of those gun butts smashed the side of his head.

CHAPTER 32

The hard jolt finally stirred Dane from unconsciousness. He lifted his head. He lay on the hard metal back of a canopied truck. He retched, coughing, trying to wipe his mouth on his sleeve. His hands were tied in front of him.

"Sexy," said Nina.

Dane rolled onto his back. Nina sat nearby on the bench seat lining the side, her hands tied as well, resting on his lap.

"You missed a great speech," she said. "Black came and told me how much smarter he is than both of us."

"I'm inclined to believe him," Dane said. He glanced at the bench across from Nina where two gunners sat, neither one of them from the force Dane had engaged.

The hard metal magnifying every jolt the truck experienced as it continued along. Dane grunted.

"They're taking us away to be shot, darling," she said. "Just you and me."

"Really?" Dane managed.

"Yup. Kinda romantic, huh?"

"I suppose." Dane inched his way to the side and struggled to sit up.

Out the rear, rolling grassy hills, trees and near total darkness. The lights of any city, of Black's mansion, were well out of range.

Dane sized up the two gunmen sitting opposite. One was younger and had a dumb look on his face. He was the soldier who took orders. The slightly older one had slicked back blonde hair, and an air of confidence.

"You must be O'Malley," Dane said to the blonde.

"Why would you guess that?"

"You look a little smarter than your friend."

O'Malley said, "I was actually expecting the British guy."

"You turkeys always do."

O'Malley and his partner kept their AIM-74 muzzles on Dane and Nina. O'Malley had a better time staying upright than his smaller counterpart, who needed one hand to stay steady when the truck hit big bumps.

Dane wondered about the cavalry. McConn and Stone. He supposed if Rachael Satastini knew of Nina's capture, perhaps she could spread the word. Dane glanced over at her. She held her head up, defiant despite the muzzles of automatic weapons trained on her belly.

The truck jolted to a stop. Dummy lurched, but O'Malley kept his weapon steady. O'Malley exited first, covered Dane and Nina; Dummy climbed out next, followed by the two captives. The cold air chilled Dane's neck. Nina shivered. The gunmen shoved them away from the truck. Dane considered the wooded area. Looking for a weapon of any kind. He spotted a thick branch on the ground. As long as it hadn't rotted from within. . .

Dane slowed his steps as O'Malley and Dummy prodded them along. When O'Malley gave him a shove, Dane sprang for the branch, swung it around, hit O'Malley's head like a baseball and wrenched the AIM-74 from his grasp. He heard Nina tangling with Dummy, both struggling over the automatic rifle. Dane whirled to the truck. The driver leveled a pistol out the window. Dane triggered a single shot that snapped back the driver's head.

Nina let out a yell. Dummy smacked her with the stock of the AIM. She fell headlong to the ground. He turned the gun on Dane. Dane fired two bursts and Dummy joined O'Malley on the ground.

Dane grabbed Nina's arm and pulled her up. The nasty welt on the side of her face was already turning red.

"Why didn't you shoot sooner?" She brushed off her clothes.

"You were doing fine."

Dane pulled the dead driver out of the truck and regarded the bloody mess spread across the cabin. He let out a breath.

"Bet you wish you'd let the driver get out first," Nina said beside him.

"Nobody's perfect."

Nina brought up the automatic rifle as three new figures converged. Stone shouted, "It's us!" and Nina lowered the weapon.

McConn, Stone and Rachael stopped to catch their breaths and survey the damage.

McConn said to Nina, "Rachael found us after they grabbed you."

"Thanks."

"Least I could do," Rachael said.

"You have a vehicle not full of blood and guts?" Dane said.

Stone gestured over his shoulder. "Back there. It's—

look out!"

A shot cracked. Rachael screamed. Dane and Nina whirled on O'Malley, who'd woken up and drawn a pistol. Dane and Nina opened fire and O'Malley's riddled body jerked as the lead slugs ripped him apart.

Dane lowered his gun and ran to Rachael, who was on the ground with Stone beside her. Her features were slack; eyes closed; blood seeping out of her chest and soaking into the dirt. Stone shook his head.

"Great," Dane hissed. He took a deep breath and backed a few steps away, letting the AIM dangle in his right hand. "Just great." He looked out at the horizon and filled his lungs again. He gazed into the horizon for a few moments. Turning back to his group, he found them looking at him, waiting.

"Who feels like burning down a mansion?"

"Try and stop us," McConn said.

"Let's sort weapons and ammo and get back there."

"What about Rachael?" Nina said.

"What about the bomb?" McConn said.

"The bomb may still be there if they didn't have a spare truck," Dane said.

"They don't," Stone said. "That's the truck we stole."

"Fine. We take Rachael with us and leave her there for when the cops arrive to clean up the mess."

"I suppose," Nina said, "it's the best we can do."

Stone drove the truck back toward Black's estate with the lights off and stopped half a mile away. Everybody piled out and lined up flat on the ground.

Nobody had a coat and the night chill bit through their clothes. The ground was cold, too, the grass damp with the first hints of dew. Dane figured it was well after two a.m.

McConn examined the grounds through night-vision binoculars. Lights still burned inside the warehouse.

"I can't see much," McConn reported. "Still plenty of guys but I don't see any guns. Wait. There's our man Teke and the foreman. There's a gunner with a rifle following Teke like a puppy. Looks like they changed the tire on the panel van."

"Be a little conspicuous with all those bullet holes," Dane said.

"They don't need to go far, I think."

Dane looked at his team. He and Nina had the pistols taken from O'Malley and Dummy while Stone and McConn toted the AIM-75 automatic rifles.

"You two take the warehouse," Dane said. "Light 'em up. Stop that van. Nina and me will deal with Mr. Black. We'll rendezvous six miles down the road."

Nina said, "Black is probably wide awake and wondering where O'Malley is."

"No, we still have some time."

"How do you know?"

"Because O'Malley hadn't dug any graves."

CHAPTER 33

■————■

Dane told McConn and Stone to wait fifteen minutes before starting their attack.

He and Nina broke off and ran in a wide circle, avoiding the warehouse and approaching the estate from the rear of the guest quarters. The windows facing them were dark. They dropped flat a few yards away and watched for signs of any troopers. None. Everybody must have been at the warehouse.

Dane rose and ran bent at the waist to the building, Nina on his heels with gun in hand. They followed the wall to a corner, heading for the side entrance of Black's mansion into the kitchen.

Dane tested the knob. It wasn't locked. They slipped into the darkened kitchen and dropped onto the tiled floor.

"Fire alarm?" Nina said.

"It worked in Zurich."

They split up and felt around for the fire alarm, bumping into fixtures and knocking over items as their hands groped in the darkness. Nina found the alarm near the interior doors that led into the rest of the house. Dane joined her. She yanked the switch. The alarm blared, a loud screech.

Spikes of pain punched through Dane's ears. A recorded voice came over a loud speaker advising guests to remain calm and proceed to their assigned evacuation point.

Dane and Nina pushed through the doorway into the main hall. Illuminated strips on the floor led from the front door, up the staircase and beyond.

Automatic weapons fire began crackling from somewhere outside, McConn and Stone joining the act.

Dane and Nina rushed up the stairs, following the lighted strips. "Rachael told me where Black's office was," Nina said.

The ghosts of battles past whispered in Dane's ear as he followed Nina. Time was quickly running out.

Stone spun the truck in a circle, kicking up a large cloud of dust, before surging ahead once again. McConn, standing in the bed of the truck, triggered bursts from the AIM, sending the warehouse crew to cover. A few gunners returned fire, their muzzles winking back, but none of the bullets found a home in either McConn's flesh or the body of the truck.

Stone made another pass, McConn strafing the building again, peppering Teke and his gunner as they ran for the van. Teke and the other man hit the dirt, hard. The gunner fired back. Stone spun around again, McConn lurching, falling hard on the truck bed. As he scrambled up, the panel van lurched to life and sped away, leaving its own cloud of dust behind. The gunman leaned out the passenger window and fired at the truck. Bullets slammed into the side, narrowly missing one of the back tires. McConn braced on the AIM on the roof and let the weapon hammer against his shoulder, but he only kicked up more dirt where the van had been.

"Go!"

Stone steered the truck after the van.

McConn rested the AIM on the roof and fired single rounds, the van zigzagging. Return fire whistled over his head. When the AIM clicked empty, he tossed the rifle aside and leaned in through the cabin's back window.

"Get as close as you can!"

"You're not gonna jump on it, are you?"

"Got a better idea? Give me your rifle!"

Stone passed back the other AIM-75 and a spare magazine. McConn stuffed the magazine in his back pocket.

Stone tried to accelerate but the bumpy terrain forced him to slow down. The paved road lay ahead. The van's lead wouldn't last long. That vehicle was much heavier than the little pick-up. McConn held his fire but kept the van in sight.

The van jolted onto the road and McConn loosed a burst as Stone gained the road, the truck jolting too but not as bad. Tires screeched on the asphalt and soon both vehicles were screaming down the road at full throttle.

The wind whipped at McConn's face. He dropped down behind the cabin as Stone started closing the gap between the truck and van.

One of the back doors of the van flew open and the gunman, laying prone, triggered a salvo that stitched through the windscreen, tearing into the empty passenger seat. McConn popped up long enough to fire back, the wind kicking the hot brass into his face. Stone swerved into the opposing lane, the gunman unable to compensate his aim. His rounds sparked on the asphalt and whined off into the night. McConn had no such handicap. Flame flashed from the AIM and stitched through the gunman.

McConn swapped magazines and stuck his head into the cabin. "Can you get closer?"

"Think so!"

McConn braced as Stone floored the pedal. The gasp closed some more. He saw Teke giving his side view mirror furtive glances, but there was nothing he could do about the pick-up. His single element of defense was leaking blood all over the floor of the van.

The truck inched closer. McConn rested the AIM on the roof and aimed at Teke. His first burst missed entirely. The second punched through the side of the van and didn't appear to hit Teke. Then Teke stuck a pistol out the window and fired blind, one of the shots coming uncomfortably close as it whined off the edge of the truck's roof. McConn fired again. The side view mirror exploded. Another burst missed Teke but punched through the windshield. Then the AIM clicked empty.

McConn tossed the weapon and leaned into the cabin.

"I'm out of quarters! Get close to the back of the van and I'll jump!"

"Are you nuts?"

"It's the only way!"

Stone let out a string of curses and swung back behind the van, quickly closing the distance. McConn climbed onto the roof. The force of the wind slammed him harder now, almost sweeping him off. He stayed flat. One of the van doors remained closed, and the stainless-steel ladder on the back of the closed door made a nice target. If he could grab the ladder and not fall off, he'd have a chance to swing directly inside the van, grab the dead gunner's weapon and use what ammunition remained on the back of Teke's head.

The front of the truck wavered within three feet of the van.

"This is it!" Stone said.

CHAPTER 34

◼━━◼

McConn skidded onto the hood, put his feet under him and leapt across. He hung in midair for a moment before the rungs were before him and he grabbed tight, crashing into the back, momentarily flailing as he lost one grip. He grasped the rungs and set for the transition inside where the crate waited, strapped to the floor of the van.

Teke swerved the van across lanes, then swerved back, McConn's feet slipping off the smooth bumper. He let out a yell as his body dangled, shoes brushing the asphalt. He lifted his legs and tried to regain footing on the bumper, but Teke kept swerving. The force of the movement pulled at McConn from all directions. One hand slipped. Stone moved the truck out of the way. McConn's other hand slipped. He hit the ground hard and tumbled furiously end-over-end.

The alarm continued blaring but the insulation in Black's office muted it a little.

Dane stood against the desk while Nina fussed with the computer, clicking on files but finding everything password protected. She let out a quiet curse each time, but finally gave up and looked at Dane.

"You sure he'll come here?"

Dane smiled. "The shooting will make him think it's a raid." He checked the captured pistol, a CZ-75 9mm, to make sure the safety was off. He needed another .45 and fast. He didn't like unfamiliar equipment, even if the CZ had a fine reputation.

Footsteps in the hallway. Hurried footsteps accompanied by the thump of a cane. The door swung open and Black, his breathing haggard, leaning heavily on his cane, entered, making for the exposed wall safe. He froze when Dane leveled the muzzle of the automatic with his gut.

"Surprise, Donovan," Dane said. "Why don't you shut that door."

Black ignored the order, his weight still on the cane. He stuck out his chin defiantly.

"It's too late to stop anything, Dane!"

"You might be surprised."

Dane lifted the CZ pistol and fired once. A neat red hole appeared between Black's eyes, the hard-nosed slug tearing through the other side to splatter part of the door and wall behind Black. Suddenly the cane couldn't support the man any longer, and he toppled headfirst onto the floor.

Dane jammed the hot pistol into the waistband of his pants. "Let's take the computer," he said, moving toward Nina, "and find a way out of here."

In the confusion of the evacuating guests, who filled the area outside the mansion like nervous chickens, Dane and Nina slipped away in the BMW they had arrived in. Neither had a cell or any way to contact McConn and Stone and hoped they'd made it to the rendezvous point unscathed. He dropped his eyes to the odometer. Four miles left.

"Steve, stop!"

Dane stomped the brakes, the headlights of the BMW shining on a man lying on his side in the road. The man wore black. Dane and Nina leapt from the car and ran to McConn, who groaned as they rolled him over.

"Oh, man, I'm hurt," McConn said. His clothes were torn, the exposed skin slashed and bleeding. Dane ran his hands along McConn's extremities.

"Nothing broken."

"My ass is broken."

"You'll live. Come on."

Dane and Nina hoisted McConn to his feet and loaded him into the back seat of the BMW. They hopped back in and Dane drove off.

McConn, resting heavily against the back seat, relayed as much of the action as he could before he passed out.

Presently the headlights flashed on the pick-up truck, waiting beside the road exactly six miles from the battleground behind them. Stone jumped out and climbed into the car.

He told the rest of the story.

"After McConn fell I kept following, but Teke got one good shot at my front tire. After that he left me behind."

Dane slammed a palm against the steering wheel.

Nothing left to do now, Dane decided, except to regroup with Lukavina and see if Black's computer held anything useful.

Derya Teke kept driving.

Nothing had gone as planned, but at least he'd escaped

with the bomb. Before leaving, he and Black had discussed how to get the bomb to Seattle as originally intended and Black suggested Teke link up with his smuggling team and let them handle the transport as previously arranged. By the time the Americans tracked down the team, they'd be long gone. The Americans wouldn't know where the bomb had gone until it detonated in Seattle.

Teke worried about his friend and hoped they polished off the American spies without trouble, but should they escape and return for Black, Teke didn't like his friend's chances of survival.

He'd learn the outcome soon enough.

It was a long flight back to the United States.

Dane and Nina had left their luggage behind, so they had to make do with the dirty and smelly outfits they'd worn the previous night. They all cleaned up as best as possible in the jet's washroom but it didn't help much. Dane telephoned ahead to Lukavina and reported they were en route and needed a few things, like weapons, and they couldn't wait for Stone's contacts to deliver this time. They needed to move fast. Lukavina directed them to a private airfield in Virginia used by the CIA and he'd have the requested items there and they could discuss the latest in the case further.

When the jet touched down, the sun blazed bright in clear blue sky. Lush greenery surrounded the airstrip, located in the Blue Ridge Mountains. Only the radar station at the end of the field, which stood tall above the tree line, indicated anything other than nature sat in those woods.

The jet taxied to a hanger where Lukavina and his second-in-command, Debra Sloane, waited, a light wind ruffling Debra Sloane's skirt. Dane opened the side door and extended the steps and let Nina exit first. She greeted Lukavina with a hug. Dane and his friend shook hands and he introduced McConn and Stone. Stone held Black's CPU.

"Let's get inside," Lukavina said. They followed him into the hanger and to a small corner room that had just enough space for a table. "Bathroom's around the corner. It has a shower. Take your time."

Dane waited with Lukavina while the others changed clothes and cleaned up in turn. The room obviously had never seen much use and signs of neglect were everywhere. The carpet had frayed corners and stains, the plain white walls looked forlorn with yellowing in some spots. A Mr. The coffee machine on a corner filing cabinet appeared older than Dane and Lukavina put together; the doors of the cabinet misaligned and crooked.

Lukavina made tea for Dane and poured himself coffee from the Mr. Coffee. He made a face when he tasted the brew.

"Nobody ever comes out here," he said.

"I don't have much to report, Len."

"Tell me what happened at Black's."

Dane gave the update, ending with, "We're no closer to Graypoole than when we started."

"Maybe that CPU will have something."

"Maybe."

"We can talk to Interpol as well."

"She was surprised we mentioned Graypoole's name," Dane said. "They weren't looking for him."

Lukavina stared into his coffee a moment, brought it to his lips, but didn't sip. He set the mug down. "Our best bet is to figure out where that bomb could be going."

"We'd be making guesses."

"But educated ones. Hang on." Lukavina called Debra Sloane, who wheeled in a cart with a laptop and other computer equipment. The CPU rode on the bottom shelf of the cart. She placed the items on the table. Lukavina hefted the CPU. Sloane connected cables to the CPU and booted the laptop.

Dane took his turn in the shower and returned in fresh clothes, feeling much better than when he'd landed. It wasn't his usual uniform, but beggars and choosers and all that.

Everybody sat around the table with Lukavina and Debra Sloane at the head, the glow of the computer screen shining on their faces.

"Black has some good stuff we'll forward to Interpol," Lukavina reported, "but nothing on Graypoole."

Dane exchanged a frown with Nina and took the chair beside her.

"What about the other thing?" Dane said.

"We did some brainstorming," Lukavina said. "We made a list of major events around the country Graypoole might target."

"You think he's going for mass casualties?"

"Mass casualties," Dane said, "and something related to economics."

Lukavina pushed the laptop Dane's way. "Have a look."

The list showed a wide variety of public events scheduled around the country in the next few weeks. Sporting events. Individual community events. Festivals. Parades. Dane was surprised they could compile such an extensive list so quickly. Nothing jumped out at him as a potential target. The whole exercise seemed silly to him as well. They still had Kader's notes, but digging through those for another lead, especially since such digging would require checking out old information to see what might still be valid, would eat time they didn't have. There was a bomb on the loose. They had to find it. Before more innocents suffered.

Dane already had too many deaths on his conscience, Lilly Klove and Rachel Satasini among them. How many more before the violence stopped? *If it ever stopped.*

"Did you see this one?" Dane said. He turned the screen back to Lukavina.

"Symposium on Cyber Security, Seattle," Lukavina said. "Why do you like it?"

"Civilians, business leaders, and government representatives," Dane said. "The capitalists Graypoole claims are the problem. All in one place. A strike there will disrupt several major companies and threaten Wall Street. It's a target he can't resist."

Nina, McConn, and Stone remained quiet.

"Change your tune?" Lukavina said.

Dane grinned.

Lukavina studied the information on the symposium provided by headquarters, and agreed with Dane's assessment. "Problem is," he added, "I can alert Homeland, but that's about all. Unless you have an idea." He raised an eyebrow at Dane.

"All we need is some equipment and gas for the jet."

"Make me a list."

CHAPTER 35

They needed most of the rest of the day to prepare but the CIA provided more clothes, weapons and ammunition, Dane receiving his requested .45 automatic, not his beloved and gone Detonics but instead a Colt Gold Cup. Nina got a new Smith & Wesson M&P Shield.

Dane and Lukavina stood outside the jet as a fuel truck attached long hoses to the wings and began pumping gas. The others were already aboard.

"I hope you're right about this," Lukavina said.

"We'll know soon enough."

The fuel truck driver disengaged the hose from the wing. Dane turned to his friend and they shook hands.

"Thanks, Len."

"Bag your limit."

Dane boarded the jet. Nina and McConn sat quietly, Nina with a drink in hand and a glass on the table beside her. McConn tapped a finger on his upper lip. Stone wrapped up a cell call and pocketed the phone. A grin split his face.

"What's up?" Dane said.

"I asked my people to send some extra goodies," he said.

"Like what?"

"You'll see. We'll make a stopover in Reno to collect."

Nina said, "Sit and have a drink, darling."

Dane joined her and she passed him the other glass.

Kassandra Ramos spooned some cat food into the dish and looked around for the stray. If he was hiding, he was very good at staying invisible. Cars drove by the house; a jogger; a young woman walking her dog. The neighborhood had been nothing but quiet since she and Ramos took the place and none of the neighbors had bothered to bring them a fruitcake. So much for civility. But she knew that was for the best.

She dropped the empty can into the trash bin and went back inside. Ramos, in the living room, dropped three sleeping bags on the floor, still rolled tight. She helped him stuff new pillows into pillow cases.

"The cat outside?"

"He's hiding," she said. At first he had been annoyed about the animal, but his attitude faded quickly. He knew she was going to feed the cat anyway so he wasn't going to waste time making a fuss.

Ramos checked his watch. "Black's people should be here soon."

"Are you hungry?"

"A little."

She whipped up toast and eggs and they sat in the breakfast nook. The kitchen table, covered with a highly-notated city map, had not been used for meals at all.

Neither spoke as they ate. Wheels were spinning inside their heads. Planning the job, following the airport shuttle day after day, and preparing for Teke's arrival had taken up so much time and effort, there was little energy left to chit-chat. Kassandra wasn't bothered by the silence. They were on a mission. They could chit-chat about trivia once the mission successfully ended.

Later that afternoon, a van pulled up in front of the house. Three men exited. Black's smugglers with the bomb. They entered the house with the suitcase. Nobody gave their name. The man in charge placed the case on the floor of the living room. The explosive was packed in foam, and he spent two hours going over how to set the bomb. He tested Ramos and Kassandra and guided them further through each step. Once they proved proficient, he wished them luck and left the house with his two associates.

Ramos and Kassandra gathered around the kitchen table and went over the map again, each step of the plan again, and watched videos they had taken of the conference center and the surrounding streets.

Now that they had the bomb, the mission felt real.

They decided to go out for the evening, and while Ramos was in the shower, Kassandra slipped out to check the cat's food dish. It was empty. As she refilled, the cat slithered from under the deck and rubbed against her wrist. Kassandra smiled and scratched the cat behind the ears. The cat arched his back and purred and when she stepped away, vigorously dived into the food.

"All right," Stone said, "it's Christmas time."

They had landed in Reno to collect Stone's goodies, and those goodies came in a knapsack. He'd left the plane and the others on the southern tarmac for twenty minutes. How he met his people, Dane didn't want to know.

As the plane taxied to take off for the final stretch of the journey to Seattle, Stone and the others stood around the table and Stone opened the pack.

"We have custom-made Interpol identification cards," he said, "and ear buds so we can talk to one another." He dumped the pile on the table.

Dane picked up the ID containing his picture. The card looked real. The leather wallet looked perfect. Dane cocked an eye at Stone. "How did you square this?"

"I'm a nefarious character," Stone said. "Probably better you don't know."

The pilot told them to find a seat while they took off. Once in the air, they examined the new items.

"I don't know how well this will pass inspection," Dane said. "If they call Paris and check on us, we'll be found out very quickly."

McConn said, "They'll be too busy, Steve." He was looking good for a man who took a hard tumble on black-top. Most of the cuts and bruises were under his clothes and healing, but a few marks on his face remained on display.

"We're going to have to use our charm, wit, and powers of persuasion to see that they stay that way," Nina said, "or I can just flash my rack."

"The solution to all of your problems, isn't it, dear?"

"Works on you all the time."

Dane's cell rang, which kept him from commenting on the muted laughter from McConn and Stone. He turned away and answered.

"Yes, Len?"

"FBI and Homeland Security are already on-scene in Seattle," he said. "The agent-in-charge is Toby O'Brien."

"Do they know about the Graypoole connection?"

"Whole ball of wax, minus the 90% still classified."

"We're working up our plan now."

"Does it include a lot of deception and sleight of hand?"

"False representation, actually."

"Even better."

"Everything is going to be fine, Len."

"Are you sure?"

"Not really," Dane said, "but it helps to keep saying so."

"I'm sending you some more intel, by the way. There are some of Graypoole's operatives we haven't been able to find included in Kader's notes, including Jose and Kassandra Ramos. If he sent Ramos and his wife to the US, and with Mueller gone it's a good bet, that's more than likely who you'll be looking for. I'm sending their dossiers."

"I'll put them on the big screen so everybody can see them."

"Stay in touch, Steve."

"Copy that."

CHAPTER 36

◼━━━◼

Steve Dane blended perfectly with the others entering the Washington State Convention & Trade Center. The main entrance was more steel-and-glass with the name of the center emblazoned above the doors. Voices and footsteps echoed inside, the polished floor reflecting what little sun streamed through the glass-walled interior. Most of the sky was gray, but nobody inside seemed to care, or maybe they were so used to the conditions they didn't notice.

Dane wore a black suit with a blue tie, part of the supplies provided by Lukavina. The suit fit, but not as well as his tailored options. However, he figured a humble Interpol man wouldn't have a tailored suit, so the off-the-rack look would help his presentation.

Nina, McConn and Stone were elsewhere on the site. Dane's job was to find the FBI agent, Toby O'Brien, and introduce the man to the idea Interpol was here too.

Dane crossed to a pair of security guards watching the crowd mill about.

He showed them his Interpol ID and gave the phony name on the card. "John Reisbach." Dane wondered if Mr.

Reisbach really existed and if so, would he object to the use of his name in such a way? What if he was a footballer with a temper? You just never knew when appropriating such things as names.

The guards looked at him with indifference as he spoke. One was older, the other younger, both rent-a-cops with as much investment in their job as a rat in his cage. "I'm here to see Toby O'Brien," Dane concluded, "the FBI agent-in-charge. Where can I find him?"

The older of the two security men deferred to the younger. The younger man pulled a walkie-talkie from his utility belt. "Lewis to Unit 4. Where's the FBI guy? We got somebody here says he's Interpol and needs to see him."

"Stand-by."

Dane waited. The older guard watched a passing woman who wore a tight blazer and pencil skirt, heels clicking on the floor, hair bouncing on her shoulders. She embraced a man on the other side of the room. The older guard looked sad.

The walkie-talkie crackled to life and whoever Unit 4 was provided directions.

The younger guard said, "Go that way, take the escalator up to the second floor, and head left down the hallway."

"Thanks."

Dane proceeded through the crowd. The escalators were straight ahead, the centerpiece of the wide area, surrounded by stone columns leading up from the floor to the upper levels. One escalator went up, the other down, and for the brave, a set of stairs waited between them. Nobody was using the stairs. Dane joined the upward flow.

He stepped off at the second floor and moved around a cluster of business people who didn't understand clustering so close to the escalator was creating a back-up of bodies who had to *sorry, excuse me* and *pardon* their way around one another. Said business people were speaking so animatedly and so oblivious to their surroundings, however, that Dane figured they probably thought they were all alone.

The empty hallway ahead beckoned to Dane. He passed closed doors on either side. Voices from an open door. Dane stopped in the doorway and tapped on the frame.

Two men in suits stood around a small table looking at a layout of the conference center. They stopped talking and turned to Dane.

One was taller than the other. He had sandy-blonde hair and wore glasses. His gray Brooks Brothers suit was standard-issue. "You Interpol?" he said.

Dane showed his credentials. "Downstairs call?"

"Downstairs was the only one that called," the man said. He took Dane's ID from him and scrutinized it. Dane sniffed. The man had probably never seen an Interpol ID before.

The man handed it back. "My office didn't say a word about your visit."

"I didn't get your name."

"Hal Morgan, Homeland Security."

The other man at the table, he little rounder in the middle with a bald patch, extended his hand. "Toby O'Brien, FBI."

Dane shook O'Brien's hand. Hal Morgan made no move to offer his.

"So what about it?" Morgan said.

"What about what?"

"My office. Not a word about you."

"I don't work for your office," Dane said.

"Not my point. We already have O'Brien here. I don't want this place overcrowded with suits looking for the same fish."

"That's the trick, isn't it? And pretty much why I'm here. Graypoole isn't only wanted by the US. I'm representing European interests so we *don't* overcrowd the place."

"Graypoole is our collar," Morgan said.

"You mean mine," O'Brien said. "I'm the only one in this room with arrest powers."

Morgan grunted. "Just you, Mr. Reisbach?"

"No. I have three associates. I came here to say hello first."

"I want to see all of them, ASAP," Morgan said. "My people need to know you're not suspects."

"Which means you suspect everybody in this building?"

"Sure, why not?"

"What kind of intel do you have pointing to this place as the target?"

"All I got is what the Pickle Factory sent over," Morgan said. "In other words, I don't got nothin'."

Dane stifled a laugh. He hadn't heard that particular nickname for the CIA in a long time. His favorite was Clowns in America.

"Hal, why don't you excuse us a moment?"

Morgan glared at O'Brien, back at Dane. "I could use a break, sure."

He stepped out.

O'Brien cleared his throat. "We're all a little edgy, I'm afraid."

"I understand. We're not here to get in your way, just observe."

"We can honestly use all the eyes we can get. Have you seen the size of this place?" O'Brien gestured to the blueprint on the table. "I have people here and here, but we're stretched thin in this area and around here."

"What about facial recognition?"

"The cameras here are only closed-circuit. I have a man in the security office looking at faces on monitors. Not very efficient. He's going to miss something."

"If Graypoole's people enter the building."

"If this building is the actual target."

"What else are you doing?"

"We've arranged for barricades out front," O'Brien said. "That's going to cause traffic problems and other inconveniences, but we'll have a detail of cops to help."

"Is there anything specific my people can help with right now?"

"Stay in touch, wander around and see if anything jumps out at you." O'Brien stuck out his hand. "Hal is pretty high-strung but he'll come around."

Dane shook. "Okay." He gave O'Brien his cell number. "Shout if you need me."

CHAPTER 37

■———■

The conference and trade show started in earnest about two hours after Dane and his team arrived. The conference center entry way and walkways became ghost towns as everybody filled the speaking rooms and display areas.

The rent-a-cops stayed at their posts while FBI agents roamed around. Three days passed with the conference going as scheduled. Agents with bomb sniffing dogs checked the parking garage in two-hour intervals. O'Brien's barricades arrived and were positioned out front to prevent vehicles from getting close to the main entrance. Traffic in front of the center backed up for blocks in every direction.

Dane, Nina, McConn and Stone observed the activity with a growing sense of dread. Dane especially. Maybe it wasn't too late to go back through the Kader file and find some cages to rattle.

Dane left the building for the garden in the back of the building, where hedgerows and trees formed a maze among a squared off concrete path. The cool air and gray clouds only made his mood worse, plus there were No Smoking signs everywhere. How could he relax without a Montecristo? He found a bench and sat down. The point of a hedge leaf poked his neck, so he moved to the left.

Nina wandered over and sat beside him. She wore a gray suit, heels, white blouse, her hair tied back in a bun, but she still managed to look ravishing. No federal agent Dane had ever seen could match her.

"Well?"

Dane shrugged.

"We can't just quit," she said.

"I know. But if we are on the wrong place, a lot of people are going to die."

"We can only wait."

"I wish I could be as calm as you."

"You mean a cold-hearted bitch?"

Dane cracked a smile.

"That's the difference between you and me," she said. "One of us has to have a little empathy."

"You don't?"

"I do, but I'm also the realist. If we're in the right spot, we can only wait for Graypoole's people to make a move. We have no idea where they are at or where to look, so we can't be proactive. The Feds seem to have the place wrapped up pretty tight. If and when something happens there will be plenty of guns on-scene. You're just afraid of being wrong."

"It was a wild guess to begin with."

"Some of the greatest events in history were based on wild guesses."

"Uh-huh."

The wind blew a little but the building didn't allow the breeze to reach them.

"I don't like that Homeland Security guy," Nina said.

"He gives me the evil eye every time we're within

spitting distance. I think he's going to be a problem."

"What kind of a problem?" Nina said.

"The kind who will want to lock us up if he thinks we're not who we say we are. What good are we then?"

She rubbed his back. "Everything will be okay."

Dane put an arm around her and squeezed. "You're becoming more like me every day."

She rested her head on his shoulder and Dane looked up at the sky. Everything was not okay. The ghosts of battles past wouldn't sleep. Graypoole would strike like a tidal wave. The only question was where.

Dane walked down the hall and entered O'Brien's office.

"You're late, Interpol," Hal Morgan said.

"And?"

The Homeland Security man glared as O'Brien, seated at the table, cleared his throat and flipped the page of a pocket notebook.

"Here's where we stand almost four days into our search," he said. We have found no bombs. We have seen no suspicious people. What we have found is one stolen car, some drugs in the bushes and various convention she-nanigans, ie: people sneaking off to have sex where they shouldn't. Do you have anything to add, Mr. Reisbach?"

"My people have come up empty as well."

"Ain't that peculiar?" Morgan said.

"Hal—"

"I'm only thinking out loud, Toby." Morgan's eyes didn't leave Dane's. Dane kept his face still. Now wasn't the time to acknowledge the sweat suddenly creeping down his neck.

Footsteps behind him. Two more men appeared in the

doorway but didn't enter the office. They effectively sealed Dane in the room.

"Our friend is a phony, Toby," Morgan said.

"What?"

"I did some checking. Interpol has never heard of nor acknowledges the existence of Mr. John Reisbach or any of his people."

O'Brien said, "Well?"

"You wouldn't have let me in if I said I was anything other than Interpol," Dane said.

"What do you mean?"

"My real name is Steve Dane. Look me up."

Morgan snapped his fingers and the two men in the doorway seized Dane's arms, and then he felt the cool touch of steel handcuffs on his wrists. One of the agents patted him down, removed his cell phone, wallet, and pistol.

"Take him downstairs while we sort this out," Morgan said.

"Who are you?" O'Brien said.

"I told you. Ask around. Call the CIA. I can't very well say more than except I'm here to help."

"Take him away."

"You're making a mistake."

"You made the mistake, pal. We'll get to the bottom of this but I think you're going to end up in a hole so deep you'll never see the sun again."

"What movie did you steal that from?"

The Homeland agents pulled Dane out of the room and gave him a shove down the hall. Being late evening, the conference attendees had vacated for their hotels for dinners out; nobody but a pair of floor security saw them as the Homeland agents pushed Dane into an elevator. The doors slid shut. The car descended to the basement level.

Concrete walls and floor, lights burning near the ceiling, very chilly. The only thing missing were the screams of others locked in the dungeon-like bottom floor.

The agents pushed Dane into a janitor's closet and shut the door, locked it.

Dane flicked on the lights with his nose and dropped into a squat, working his bound wrists over his bottom and legs and letting out a sigh when he had his hands in front of him again. The closet was crammed with cleaning supplies, mops, buckets, packages of micro-fiber towels. Dane found an open spot on the wall and sat. The floor was cold and immediately made his rear end sore.

At least they weren't tying him to a chair to whack his balls with a carpet beater. There were worse things than spending time in the company of bleach and Simple Green.

They'd round up the others, too, unless Nina, McConn and Stone were a little faster on the uptake.

But why the closet? They should have had police standing by to take him to the station for holding. Would Morgan take the time to check his "real" story or just leave him there long enough for the cavalry to show up and drag him to Guantanamo?

He sat alone in the quiet of the closet for a while, then heard commotion in the hallway. Muted voices became louder. Nina, yelling and cursing in Russian.

Dane shook his head. "Not gonna help, honey."

The struggling continued past his door and another door in the hallway slammed.

That left McConn and Stone.

But his hopes quickly faded. More noises in the hall but less talking. McConn voice broke through, though, something about the real bad guy still on the loose. The Homeland goons weren't listening. They had their terror-

ists and now it was beer time. Two more slammed doors.
How many rooms were in the hallway, anyway?

At least they were near each other and if Dane could
get out, they'd be easy to find.

Nothing to do but wait and see.

Meanwhile, Graypoole had a bomb set to go off.
Somewhere.

And Dane might be truly powerless to prevent the
explosion.

He sat with his face a grim mask.

CHAPTER 38

———◆———

Toby O'Brien said, "And just how long do you intend to leave them down there?"

"Until this situation is under control," Morgan said.

"You aren't even going to check his story?"

"What story? We're looking for suspicious people. They fit the bill. They are contained. Now we just have to find their bomb."

"What if you're wrong?"

"How would you know?"

"I've been around long enough," O'Brien said, "to lose my hair doing this job. I think my instincts are pretty good."

"Fine. You make some calls. I'm going to go look for a bomb."

Morgan left the office and didn't bother to close the door.

O'Brien sat at the table and shook his head. He took out his cell phone and started to call headquarters, then decided to dial somebody else. He had connections at CIA from his friendship with a former employee. Maybe he could ask them directly since Dane had made the suggestion.

The line answered on the fifth ring.

"Debra Sloane, please," O'Brien said. "Extension 2408."

It was a short wait and then Debra Sloane, number two at the counter-terrorism division, answered. "Yes?"

"Deb, it's Toby O'Brien. I'm in Seattle and I got a question for you. . ."

Dane eventually dozed off but jerked awake when a key slipped into the closet lock.

He stood as the door opened. Toby O'Brien stood there with two agents behind him.

"I told you Morgan was a hard case," he said.

"Uh-huh."

"I made a phone call. Does the name Debra Sloane mean anything to you?"

"Maybe."

"I know her. I asked about you. She had to get permission from her boss, but she vouched for you."

"Great."

And Lukavina would never let him hear the end of it. Especially if Graypoole's bomb went off.

O'Brien said, "I'm letting the four of you go. I'll deal with Morgan. This stays between us. Let's get your team out of here and back on the job."

Kassandra Ramos peeked through the curtain and her heart sank.

The cat had not been outside the night before when she brought out the food dish and the food had dried out, untouched, overnight. She replaced it with fresh food after her morning shower and it still remained.

Where was the kitty?

She looked out the window for a while, hoping, and then she heard Ramos behind her.

"It's time," her husband said.

Ramos drove to SeaTac, parking the car in the short-term lot and lugged the suitcase containing the bomb to a shuttle stop at the edge of the parking lot. To make it look good, Kassandra carried her luggage as well. Jets roared overhead as they touched down; others climbed high as they took off. The overcast sky didn't seem to bother the pilots, who broke through the clouds with practiced ease. Kassandra watched the planes and tried to get her mind off the cat. They wouldn't be returning to the house. She hoped the next tenants would care for the kitty cat too.

The shuttle bus presently arrived, the young driver not saying hello as they boarded. The bench seat lining the side of the bus was hard molded plastic without a pad. It wasn't uncomfortable, but also not where one wanted to sit for a long period.

They stowed their luggage under the seat.

The bus waited twenty minutes. Nobody else arrived.

Kassandra breathed a sigh of relief. They only had the driver to contend with. He looked like a college kid and had skinny arms showing no real muscle mass. He wouldn't put up a fight.

The driver put the vehicle in gear and started off. He merged into city traffic as he left the airport property and then Ramos reached under his jacket for a pistol.

They neared a shopping center with a full parking lot. Ramos left the seat and went to the driver.

"Sit down, please," the driver said.

Ramos jabbed the gun into his neck. "Pull into that

parking lot and go behind the store."

Kassandra took out her own gun and switched to the bench across from where she sat. The driver, shaking, complied, his lips pressed together. He slowed and followed the order, driving the bus behind a Safeway, passing the loading dock, and continuing almost to the other side of the property. Ramos told him to stop near a set of Dumpsters.

The driver stopped.

"Up."

Ramos stepped back to allow the driver to stand. Ramos grabbed him by the shirt collar, pulled him back a few steps and smashed the pistol over his head. The driver collapsed in a heap in the back of the bus. Ramos handed Kassandra his gun and sat behind the wheel.

Ramos drove forward and turned right as the wheels touched the street.

Not much further now.

And nobody to stop them.

Dane and his team checked in with O'Brien at nine a.m. sharp. Hal Morgan didn't say a word to him. Dane ignored him. He split the team up to cover the four sides of the convention center. Nina took the front, McConn and Stone the sides of the building and Dane scouted the rear.

Ignoring the No Smoking signs, Dane lit a Montecristo and made his rounds leaving a trail of smoke behind him. The closet conundrum he hadn't needed. What did they miss because Morgan had an attitude? He told himself to relax. He wasn't the only one looking.

He wandered around the rear the building, checking the loading dock, where the cafeteria crew hustled to unload semis with the day's supply of fresh food.

The sidewalk and street behind the building, not barricaded, looked normal. Dane smiled at a lady who held at least six dogs of various size and breeds on many leashes. The dogs seemed perfectly happy.

As he dropped the finished Montecristo in the street, Nina's voice came over his ear bud:

"Eyes on target."

Dane ran for the rear entrance. "What do you see?"

"Jose and Kassandra Ramos. They're crossing the street and continuing west away from the conference center. Heading for 7th Street, other side of the movie theater."

"Don't engage till we get there. Guys, do you copy?"

McConn and Stone acknowledged as Dane pulled open one of the rear entrance doors and started running. He dialed O'Brien on his cell and gave him the update.

"Two suspects in the vicinity, get everyone you have checking the perimeter!"

"Where are the suspects?"

"Crossing the street in front of the building heading west. My people are closing in."

"On it. Back-up coming behind you."

CHAPTER 39

———◆———

The Sketchers Nina wore made running a breeze. She let Ramos and Kassandra get across the street, then hustled after them, hidden in a flow of convention guests heading for the corner coffee shops on that side. Ramos and Kassandra cut between the ACE Theater and a coin and stamp shop. Seventh Street lay beyond, with a quick right taking them to Pike Street where they might have a car. Nina ran a little faster, stopping and starting as she found cover to let the targets keep a little ahead.

McConn's voice in her ear: "Nina, I'm opposite of you, Pike and Seventh."

"They're heading your way." Nina moved from an alcove and back onto the pavement as Ramos and Kassandra indeed made the right and started for 7th Street.

Nina reached 7th where McConn joined her and they watched the suspects walk down Pike. Holding hands, no less.

"What's ahead?" Nina said.

McConn consulted a map on his cell phone. "Variety of shops and Westgate Park."

Dane and Stone chimed in. "Across the street, you two."

Nina and McConn looked. Dane and Stone waved. They began moving parallel to each other with Ramos and Kassandra directly ahead.

Dane's cell chirped.

"What is it, Toby?" Dane huffed as he talked and walked.

"We found a stray airport shuttle that shouldn't be here. The dogs are—"

The ground shook with tremendous force. Dane and Stone landed hard as the air around them seemed to vanish, leaving them not only gasping, but feeling the shockwave of a bomb blast lighting the sky. A towering cloud of smoke filled the air where the convention center stood, the ever-widening plume spewing chucks of debris all around. Dane rolled onto his back, still gasping, and gazed at the smoke.

"Up!" he shouted. He didn't even know if the team could hear him. "Take 'em now!"

Dane broke into a sprint. Stone followed behind. They cut across the street, dodging stopped cars, the drivers' horrified expressions focused on the explosion.

Nina and McConn caught up as Dane and Stone reached the sidewalk and that's when Ramos and Kassandra started running, too. The couple split up, Kassandra rushing across the street. Nina said she'd follow the woman and crossed after her. Dane, McConn and Stone stayed with Ramos as he cut left on 6th Street and ran headlong through the confused pedestrians either running away or running toward the blast location. He did not appear to have a weapon in hand, Dane noticed as he drew the Colt Gold Cup .45 auto.

McConn and Stone cut through an alley to try and get ahead of Ramos. Dane remained in pursuit. O'Brien's back-up wouldn't be coming, he knew. It was all up to them. Had O'Brien survived the blast?

Smoke and dust from the explosion drifted over-head, filling the street, as Dane continued his pursuit, Ramos slowing a little as he dodged obstacles. Ramos tripped on a pothole and fell. Dane finally reached him as the man rolled onto his back. That's when Dane saw the pistol. Dane didn't stop running and instead leaped over Ramos, tumbling to the ground on the other side and going into a roll. As he came up, Ramos was running the other way, heading for an alley. Dane bolted after him. Ramos entered the alley, but now McConn and Stone were entering from the other side, guns up. Ramos raised his weapon and braced to fire. Dane fired twice. Both shots punched through Ramos' back. He screamed, arching, head going back and arms going high as he fell. His pistol landed first.

Dane and his partners rushed to the body. Dane felt for a pulse. None. Ramos' eyes, however, remained opened.

When Nina saw Kassandra Ramos was leading her toward the Nordstrom shop, she figured they could fight and do some shopping at the same time. Or fight *while* shopping. A tussle over a purse maybe. Or shoes. Everybody would understand women fighting over shoes.

Kassandra Ramos kept snapping her head back to check the pursuit, unintentionally slowing her down. Eventually Kassandra ducked behind a car and fired a string of rounds at Nina, all going wide and bouncing off the asphalt. Nina heard people screaming around her, but her eyes stayed on Kassandra. She held her fire, taking cover behind a car as well. Staying low, she moved in a crouch along the sidewalk. Kassandra was still watching the street. She raised her head just enough to look around and that's when Nina rushed forward and leaped over the hood of the car Kassandra hid behind. As they collided, Nina grabbed for the woman's neck.

They rolled into the street. Kassandra continued the roll, breaking Nina's grasp. As Nina tried to get up, Kassandra lashed out with a kick, connecting with Nina's mouth. Nina fell back and rolled away. Rising, she spat blood and launched a series of kicks and punches at the other woman, who expertly blocked and dodged and lashed out with a return roundhouse snapping Nina's body in a full circle. Her face met the pavement again. Kassandra ran off. Nina spat more blood and this time a curse. She rose to continue the pursuit, but there was now no sign of Kassandra.

There were, however, plenty of sirens wailing in the air.

Kassandra ran.

She wasn't alone as other pedestrians were either running to the explosion or away from it. Police and emergency vehicles screamed along Pike Street, up ahead. She took refuge in a dress shop, breathing hard as she leaned against the wall beside the door. The frightened clerk rushed from behind the desk.

"Are you okay? What happened out there?"

"Building blew up," Kassandra said, trying to catch her breath. Her sides hurt. She slid down the wall to the floor.

The clerk, a young girl around sixteen, brought her some water. Kassandra took a long drink.

"I need to find my husband," she said, starting to get up.

"You're hurt, stay here. I'll call an ambulance."

Kassandra pushed away the girl's offered hand and stood. "I need to find my husband," she said again, and went out the door.

She followed 6th Avenue south, intersecting with Pike Street, the last place they had been together. She stood at the corner. Smoke still hung in the air; the cloud from the convention center had yet to dissipate. The closer she got, the louder the sirens and assorted chaos of the recovery. They'd seal off and evacuate surrounding streets soon.

She leaned against the corner of a building and tried to settle down. Think. She had to find Jose but she also had to report to their employer. She felt around her pockets for her cell phone and pulled it from the left side. The screen was cracked from the fight, but it still functioned. She dialed a number.

"Yes?"

"Mission accomplished," she said.

"Very good," said Mason Graypoole. "Where are you?"

"Near the scene, I need to find Jose before we reach the rendezvous."

"Where is Jose?"

"We got separated."

"Follow the protocol, Kassandra. He'll find you."

"I need to find my husband!"

"Do not screw around, Kassandra. We're at the island. I'm sending you the coordinates. Get here as soon as you can."

She didn't say okay or good-bye, ending the call before Graypoole said anything more.

She ran across Pike. She'd seen Jose running this way when she stole one last look over her shoulder when they split.

Activity ahead. People loitering and talking about what

happened, what some who ventured to the scene saw. Kassandra slowed and wandered past them in a daze. Her head spun a little. She hurt in several places. Whoever that woman had been, some of her punches and kicks had landed solidly.

She kept walking, almost stumbling at a pot hole. She stopped in the street. Somebody came over; she brushed him off. As she turned, she saw an alley, and the floor of the alley didn't look right.

She let out a wail halfway there, falling beside her husband's body and sobbing onto his chest, her body convulsing. At least his eyes were closed, she saw, when she finally looked at his face.

And then the sobbing suddenly stopped.

A foot shuffled behind her.

She turned. A man stood at the mouth of the alley holding a gun. Another footstep behind her. Two more men. And then a woman, stepping out of an alcove. The same woman she'd fought near Nordstrom. Kassandra pressed her lips together. The woman held her pistol casually but steady.

"Don't try it, honey," Nina said. "You'll end up like your old man."

CHAPTER 40

———————◆———————

Kassandra let out a wail and lunged for Nina, who stepped aside and fired twice. Kassandra felt the bullets tear through her. Two more shots—from behind. She fell face first. Pressing her hands into the concrete, she started to push herself up, wedged a knee under her. Her eyes never left those of the woman, who leveled her pistol and fired again.

She dropped again and this time didn't move.

"Game girl," Nina said.

The cell phone in Kassandra's pocket chimed.

Nina reached into Kassandra's jeans to take out the phone, using her fingertips to avoid getting blood on her hands.

"Move out," Dane said, grabbing Nina's arm as she worked the phone.

"This is juicy, Steve," she said, trying to keep up as the men moved ahead of her. She slipped her hand around Dane's left elbow.

"Wow, a private island," she said, reading. "Looks like Graypoole sent the location. I bet we can have a good party there. Should we bring chips and dip?"

"We'll bring something," Dane said as they exited the other side of the alley.

What Dane didn't voice was his concern for people at the bomb site. How many dead? How many injured? A cacophony of emergency sirens drifted through the air. People better equipped than he to help were on the way. It was one of those moments where he felt powerless to contribute anything of value, as powerless as he'd been to keep Lilly Klove safe from a hail of bullets.

He'd sworn at the girl's grave there would be no more victims, but he should have known better than to make a promise he couldn't keep when dealing with madmen bent on destruction.

But he would settle accounts with those responsible.

The street was clear of traffic and the smoke hung heavy in the air.

Dane moved to the corner and looked down the street at the carnage. He couldn't see much with all the smoke and dust, but he could hear people yelling and calling for help.

"We need to go, Steve," Nina said.

McConn said, "If we go west that's probably our best bet for avoiding police."

"We need to go back and help," Dane said.

"Dammit, Steve—"

He turned to Nina. "Go if you want to. But this is what I do."

Dane started running toward the building and didn't look back. He knew the others would be right behind him.

Dane didn't bother to call Lukavina, or return the CIA man's calls, as Stone's jet soared at 20,000 feet. He sat in a chair by a window, his face washed of most of the accumulated grit from the explosion, his clothes still dirty. The others were just as dirty. The jet's small bathroom sink couldn't repair all the damage.

Dane stared at the carpet not feeling much good to anybody. There had been plenty of injured to stabilize, albeit crudely, while they waited for paramedics; there were plenty of dead and dying as well. He wasn't sure about the others, but every last breath of the victims fueled his quest to stop such things from happening again. The problem was, no matter how many of the enemy he killed, they were always quickly replaced. How long could he keep going? How long till the opposition caught him when he wasn't looking and ended *his* life?

Sometimes it all seemed like a waste of time.

And that's when he vowed never to quit, as he often did. Because if he stopped, the madmen would run free.

Stone made a flurry of calls. They needed a plane they could jump out of, SCUBA gear, and assorted small arms. The best he could arrange was a C-130 at an airstrip in Florida but everything they needed would be there when they arrived.

While Stone made his calls, Dane, Nina and McConn looked at Graypoole's island on a computer map. The co-ordinates provided by Graypoole on Kassandra's phone gave the exact location.

It was an old photograph, McConn surmised, since it didn't show any signs of life, but it at least gave them an idea of what they were looking at, and it wasn't hard to guess where any structures would sit. It was close enough to Spain to qualify as part of their territory, but the Spaniards had apparently found nothing worthwhile to do with the land.

Everybody tried to sleep on the remainder of the journey but Dane couldn't keep his eyes closed for the longest time. That was one thing they didn't have. Once Graypoole realized Kassandra Ramos was DOA and his transmission of his location was now in the hands of the authorities, he'd vanish. Dane didn't want to tell Lukavina until they were well ahead of any response official powers could muster.

The six-hour flight finally ended at the Florida airstrip where they saw the C-130 Hercules waiting for them. The surrounding forest told Dane they were in the middle of nowhere and the less he asked about the airstrip the better off he'd be.

Two crates sat aboard the cargo area of the C-130, the long and wide steel tube stripped of even the bare essentials Dane had spent so much time in. Small port windows looked fogged over and the canvas benches along either side of the fuselage always left one with a sore bum. Relief finally came when one got to jump out of the goddamn thing.

The crew master, a short kid with a crew cut, his military cap on backwards, helped get the crates open. Among the weapons inside were the SCUBA suits and parachutes Dane requested. Each of them took a suit, SCUBA gear, parachute, fighting knife, and an M-4 automatic rifle with a collapsible stock. Separate boxes within one of the crates held ammunition, magazines and assorted timed explosives.

Once the flight crew finished their inspection, the engines fired and the C-130 began to taxi.

"Where are you?" Lukavina said.

Dane had the phone volume up all the way and still had a hard time hearing.

"Somewhere over the Atlantic, about four hours from the target."

"What target?"

"The one I'm sending you now. Graypoole's headquarters." He explained how they had acquired the location.

"And when were you planning to tell me about this?"

"When we were close enough to get there before you," Dane said.

"One of these days you're going to be too smart for your own good, Steve."

"But not today," Dane said.

Dane ended the call before Lukavina said more, but he sent the coordinates with a smile. He didn't blame his friend for being miffed, but he would calm down once he pondered the bigger picture.

The crew chief shouted for them to get ready. Dane, Nina, McConn and Stone gathered near the ramp, each pulling waterproof night-vision goggles over their eyes.

As the rear of the C-130 opened into the pitch black of the night sky, the only sign they weren't jumping into a black abyss were wisps of clouds here and there. A chill crept up Dane's back that had nothing to do with the cold wind filling the cabin. They were jumping into the dark. The same dark he'd seen in Belgium.

But when the crew master said go, Dane didn't hesitate. He leapt from the plane with the others trailing behind him and the four figures slashed through the air, wind thrashing at their bodies. Dane's night vision gear helped him see where they were going, but that didn't help the flash of disorientation he sensed every few seconds. The wind wanted to turn him upside down and around; he used his arms and legs to stay level, and the battle never ceased. Dane didn't have to like sky diving. He only had to do it when the job required.

They remained in free-fall for an agonizing three minutes. Dane checked the luminous dial of his watch and stole a glance over his shoulder. Stone's parachute billowed open. A few seconds later, McConn pulled his rip cord and air filled his canopy. Nina next. When gravity had provided the required space between Dane and his lady, he pulled his own rip cord and waited for the violent tug on his upper body that meant the parachute was fully open. The tug happened as expected, pulling on his torso and shoulders like a semi at full throttle and a grunt of pain escaped his lips. Still gasping a little, Dane grabbed the risers dangling beside his head and began stabilizing his descent to the ocean below.

At least he told himself it was the ocean. To his eyes, it was nothing but a wave of darkness that soon swallowed him and his team.

CHAPTER 41

———◼———

The moment they hit the water, the team shed their parachute gear and began swimming. Each had a compass and the coordinates in case they became separated, but, staying on Dane, they swam toward their objective and reached the beach twenty minutes later.

The team remained flat on the sand, icy water washing over them, wave after wave. It provided cover while they looked around. Typical beach. Lots of sand. About twenty yards from the water, the rocky face of raised ground. Nothing visible beyond that. Dane looked up and down the beach. No sign of a patrol. A small cave lay ahead in the rock face; he pointed it out and moved forward, water dripping from his wet suit as he padded across the sand, the swim fins kicking up bursts of sand in his wake. The others followed. They ducked into the cave as far back as they could and began shedding SCBUA gear, lacing boots and preparing weapons after removing their protective covering. The ground wasn't level and Dane leaned against the rough wall for support as he locked a magazine into his M-4.

"Everybody splits like we planned," he said softly. "Five minute intervals."

Stone took off first, then McConn. Nina gave Dane a salty wet peck on the cheek and departed. Dane let out a breath and followed six minutes later. He didn't want to leave the cave. It felt like the last safe place. He couldn't shake the vision of the dark. But as Dane crawled up the rock face and ran along the raised ground, boots thumping on the hard earth, the ghosts of battles past reminded him that there was no room for fear with so much at stake and so many lives lost. The battle had to end here. Tonight.

Dane ran on.

The first patrol crossed his path about 150 yards from the beach.

The heavy woods provided excellent cover as Dane allowed nature to absorb him. He lay flat, surrounded by thick leaves and poking branches. The three-man patrol moved along a well-trodden path, appropriately separated, communicating via radio. He hadn't expected that. The natural cover would make it hard to see the gunmen during a fight, which gave them plenty of time to radio headquarters for back-up. Such a request would alert Graypoole to their presence on the island. No more surprise. He had no plans to engage for that reason but remained ready to fight in case they saw him. Dane waited long after the trio had passed before he started moving again.

Each of them had an objective. Dane wanted an observation point over the control center or main working area; the others were looking for places to plant their bombs. Radio towers. Radar stations. Anything that, once gone, left the enemy crippled. The computer map had shown them nothing of the sort, so they had to find it the hard way. Enlisting the CIA's help might have provided better intelligence on what to expect, but Dane's desire for operational security, or, rather, his desire for revenge, overrode that idea. The presence of the troops at least confirmed they were in the right place.

Dane stayed off the paths he found, the obvious routes of the patrols and kept to the thicket, weaving around trees and treading as quietly as possible over leaves and branches. It was slow going. Sweat tricked down his neck, his combat blouse sticking to his back. He breathed slowly and stopped and dropped every few feet to listen. No other patrols so far. Did they have a light force on purpose, or was it something to keep the men busy? How secure did Graypoole believe he was on this private island?

The ground began to slope upward and Dane took longer breaks. When he reached the top, drenched with sweat, he dropped flat again and looked over the side of the hill into the valley below.

About 200 yards down, the ground had been cleared to allow construction of a one-story building topped with aerials and a radar dish. Set perpendicular was another building, this one resembling the barracks found at every military base worldwide. Was this the nerve center? Using his night vision goggles, Dane scanned the surrounding area. The building backstopped against the face of a hill. Dane could not detect if anything strategic sat atop that hill. Near the barracks, on a pair of adjoining landing pads, were two Bell helicopters. One had a machine gun sticking out of the cabin.

Off to the left, closer at 50 yards, he spotted a primary target. A circular bungalow with a railed deck. It rested on the sloping side of the hill, supported on thick beams.

Two men were on the deck, talking. Dane zoomed in. An older man he did not recognize and a younger, taller man. Mason Graypoole.

Dane examined the slope before him. If he could work his way down and find a firing position across from the bungalow, the snake might lose its head.

He started at a crawl, pushing through the undergrowth, wary of trip wires and booby traps. He found none. A fallen log provided the position he wanted. Readying the M-4, he rested against the log and sighted along the barrel. A scope would have been nice, but improvisation was a commando's bread-and-butter.

The two men continued their conversation, the older man leaning against the rail with his arms folded. He did most of the talking. Dane wondered about Graypoole's somber expression as he placed the sights on the man's left eye.

Dane slipped his finger through the trigger guard and started to apply pressure.

The spotlight hit him, lighting up his hiding place like daylight, associated yells filling the night. A string of rounds crackled below, nipping at the foliage around him. Dane held Graypoole in his sights and fired but before the bullet found its mark, Graypoole and the other man had dived inside the bungalow.

Dane swung the M-4 down the hill. Troops were already converging, charging through the growth, some with dogs. The barking dogs seemed louder than the gunshots. Dane fired a burst, then pivoted and charged up the slope with his legs pumping like pistons.

Good news, he could keep the force occupied so the others could find their own targets. Bad news, who knew how long he could run?

More shots struck around him, fired blind and for effect, but Dane forged ahead, leaves and branches whipping at his face, the threat of tripping over a branch or log ever present in his mind. He leaped over a fallen tree trunk, almost slipped on leaves when he landed, but kept going. The barking dogs faded somewhat. But they were still back there.

Then he heard the helicopter.

CHAPTER 42

—■————■—

The whipping rotor blades drowned out the dogs. He found cover for a moment and listened. The chopper flashed overhead, a spotlight burning from the canopy. The beam of light shined through the trees. They wouldn't be able to see much, but maybe there was a clearing up ahead that they expected him to reach. The dogs again. Getting closer. Dane left his hiding spot and ran. The chopper buzzed over-head, the spotlight breaking through the tree canopy here and there.

Dane's wrist compass showed he was heading east.

No clearings yet, but he did find a wide pathway, probably one of the paths used by the patrols. He started following it, grateful for a few moments of not having his face and body lashed, but he couldn't stay. The chopper buzzed overhead once more.

The forest thinned out and he crossed from hard ground to sandy beach. Ahead sat a row of motor boats tied to a jetty. Each boat had a machine gun mounted in the rear. Hello, Dolly. Dane ran faster, his boots sinking into the sand, legs and lungs straining. If he could lead the pursuing force off the island entirely, that would give Nina, McConn and Stone a better chance.

He leapt aboard one of the boats and cast off the lines. The chopper roared overhead, a gunner firing from the open cabin, the hammering thunder of rounds stitching the jetty but missing the boat. Dane swiveled the mounted gun around to fire at the rear of the helicopter and triggered a burst. The Browning .50-cal rocked against the steel post holding it aloft, but the shots missed as the chopper sharply banked to the left.

Single shots nicked the boat and zipped overhead as the pursuing force and the dogs reached the beach. Dane swung the Browning that way. He triggered a long burst, moving the barrel left to right, kicking up big clouds of sand and driving most of the troops flat. He ran to the steering wheel, the key already in the ignition. He pressed the starter and the engines roared to life. Dane gave the throttle a push. The motor chugged, the rear of the boat dipped, and sent a wave out in either direction that rocked the other boats as it rocketed away from the jetty.

The night's cold stung Dane's face, bits of water striking his skin, but he was away, traveling deep into the dark and if he could get rid of that chopper and double back, he could leave the troops wandering aimlessly while he and his crew tore apart Graypoole's hideout.

The chopper swept around behind him, the spotlight creating a circle of light around the entire boat. Dane tore the .45 from leather and fired at the canopy as the machine gunner let loose a string of fire that cut through the front of the boat. Dane fired twice in return, looked over his shoulder to correct his aim and fired twice more. The chopper backed off a little. Dane cut the wheel right, the spotlight trying to follow. As he steered parallel with the chopper, he fired two more blasts from the .45 with little or no effect. He cut under the chopper as it tried to swing his way, reversing course, but now he was heading toward shore and the troops that had chased him had found their own boats and were speeding his way.

Dane shoved the throttle forward, the rear end dipping again, the nose of the boat rising as he flew headlong into the line of boats before him. They scattered to avoid him, crashing into one another and Dane slowed a little as he neared the beach. He turned left, aiming for the coastline, following it as close as he could without running aground.

The chopper relentlessly stayed on his tail, finally catching up as he ran the boat along the coastline, the door gunner blasting away. The bullets cut the air over Dane's head, smacked into the body of the boat. Dane followed the right-hand drift of the coastline and turned the wheel, his mind racing for a solution. He couldn't outrun the chopper. He couldn't hide. The aircraft would act as a beacon for the other boats once they organized again. Dane ran to the mounted machine gun and swung it around. He fired at the chopper's underbelly, raised his aim to the engine. Smoke began pouring out of the back. He'd scored a hit, but the machine wasn't slowing down. It circled again, trailing smoke. The door gunner fired a burst that stitched through the floor and side and smacked the gas tank with a loud thwack. Dane zeroed his sight and fired. The windshield caved under the impact of the bullets and the chopper dropped nose first into the water. The explosion lit the night, flame shooting skyward, chunks of debris splashing in the water and sailing over Dane's head.

The other boats rounded the curve. Closing fast.

The motor still chugged but without much life. Dane pushed the throttle forward, but the motor only responded with half the enthusiasm as before. His gas tank gauge read near empty. The machine gunner not only blasted his fuel supply but damaged his engine. Dane spun the wheel toward shore, coaxing as much power as he could from the motor. When he reached the sand, he grabbed his M-4 and leaped over the side.

He trudged over the wet sand, his boots unable to get any traction and that cost him time. The pursuing boats raced closer, the barking dogs more audible as the engines cut off. Dane looked back once. Three dogs launched themselves from the boats and charged at him like heat-seeking missiles. Dane finally reached dry sand and took two steps before his left foot struck drift wood and he tumbled face first, the M-4 flying from his grasp. He snatched the .45 and rolled over, taking aim at the lead dog. The animal's eyes glinted in the low light of the moon, his gray coat thick, muscles contracting beneath his fur. Dane tightened on the trigger but by then they were on top of him, mouths open and when those mouths closed on flesh, Steve Dane screamed.

CHAPTER 43

Dane's puffy eyes opened. His right cheek rested on scratchy carpet. His arms had been wrenched behind his back, both wrists secured with a plastic tie. He felt neither arm, but the combat blouse was torn, bite marks on exposed skin still bleeding a little. A coating of dry sweat and bits of sand clung to the rest of him. The pain from the bites hadn't come to life yet; it would presently, but Dane saw another sight that took his mind off his condition.

Mason Graypoole sat a few feet away in a leather chair, legs crossed. He shook his head.

"We finally meet," Graypoole said. "And once again I've come out on top. You should have picked another career. If you were on a football team, they'd have traded you."

Dane said nothing through his swollen lips. Pain flared through his body. The dogs had bit his legs and arms. The bites throbbed.

"Don't worry about rabies," Graypoole said. "I wouldn't put my men at risk with rabid dogs. I spend too much money on the troops for that. But those bites may become infected, you know. Also, I don't have detention cells in this facility, so this suite in the living quarters will have to suffice." Graypoole smiled. "Hope you don't mind."

Dane was content to breathe.

"Are you the advance force or something? I sure hope there are others more competent than you. Of course, we haven't found any yet. I'm beginning to think the US has no idea how to respond to me."

Dane blinked.

"We keep checking the radar for any ships or planes. Nothing so far. We wouldn't see stealth fighters, but none have arrived yet. I think you're all alone here, pal."

Dane let out a little laugh.

"I think you're going to be here a little while, until I can figure out what to do with you."

Graypoole rose, turned for the door; with his hand on the knob, he looked back and said, "What I want is a final showdown. Maybe I'll make a video with you and taunt them a little. They have to show up sometime." Graypoole opened the door and went out.

Dane breathed into the carpet. The door closed quietly. He finally let out a groan. But he forgot the pain when a thought occurred to him.

Where were Nina, Stone and McConn?

Nina watched two troopers drag Dane into the housing unit, his boots clunking up the steps, his body slack. Obviously unconscious but cut and bleeding as well. Well now they had two objectives and she wouldn't leave until the baddies were done for and she had Steve back beside her. She lay in a hiding spot on the slope behind the troops' quarters and let out a breath.

Slight movement to her left. She turned slowly, bringing the M-4 around with her. Stone whispered her name.

"Here," she said.

He crawled on knees and elbows beside her with McConn slithering close as well. The leaves surrounding them were wet, the ground soft. Mud covered their combat clothes and packs.

"Where's Steve?" McConn said.

She pointed at the barracks.

"It's up to us then," Stone said.

"I've found the radar tower," Nina said.

"We located a power station," McConn said. "If we can blast that, this whole place will go dark."

"Okay," Nina said. "Todd, lights out is your signal to hit the barracks. Dev, take the power station. I'll knock out the radar."

Stone departed as quietly as he arrived. Nina told McConn good luck as he moved out. McConn checked his weapon and began the agonizing slow move down the slope to the base of the mountain where it met the rear of the barracks. The voices of the troopers inside drifted his way; three stood guard around the front steps. He hoped it wouldn't be a long wait before the lights went out.

The two troopers inside the radar station left the door propped open with a rock. They talked quietly as the glow of the screens filled the shack-like structure with the array of dishes and antenna adjacent.

Nina crept closer, staying at the edge of the foliage and the clearing the radar station sat in. Wind rustled the leaves around her. She placed her M-4 on the ground and took out her silenced Smith & Wesson. She raised the gun and fired once, twice. Both troopers slid out of their chairs and onto the floor with head shots, the bloody mess left behind covering the floor.

Nina holstered the pistol, slung her rifle and unloaded two bricks of explosive from her pack. She placed one brick at the base of the shack, the other at the edge of the fence surrounding the dish and antenna array. She set the timers for five minutes each and beat it out of there, following the path she had taken to the top, almost sliding onto her bottom when she stepped on a flattened leaf slick with moisture rather than solid ground.

She made her way back toward the barracks. McConn would need covering fire.

When the bombs went off, the flash of the explosions lit the night, the concussions following a moment later. An alarm started to blare, a loud klaxon and then another pair of explosions shook the island. Lights around the compound snapped off. Hand-held spotlights popped on as troopers tried to discover where the attack originated.

At the barracks, McConn fired from cover, stitching the three troopers near the front steps before they knew what hit them. Their bodies fell and McConn, his night vision guiding him, stepped over the bodies and up the steps and into the barracks.

An open area, beds and lockers on either side, troopers in various stages of undress confused and trying to get dressed and grab weapons. McConn broke left up some steps, turning right at the landing and going up another flight. Carpeted floor, three closed doors. McConn tried the closest on his left. Locked. "Steve!"

"In here!"

McConn shifted to the door on his right, giving the knob a solid kick. Shouts below; heavy footsteps; nobody coming up the stairs. All troops were mustering outside. When he heard the crackle of automatic weapons fire, McConn knew Stone and Nina had returned from their individual tasks.

McConn found Dane on the carpet, dropped beside him. He set his rifle down and used a knife to cut the bonds holding Dane's wrists. As Dane shook his hands to get the circulation going, McConn handed him the knife and picked up the M-4. He stood near the doorway, watching the stairwell, while Dane cut the straps on his ankles.

More shouting below. Heavy footsteps coming up the stairs. Somebody remembered Dane after all. McConn shouldered the M-4. As the two troopers cleared the landing, he squeezed the trigger. The long burst cut both men almost in two, sending their bodies back down the stairs in a bloody and mangled heap. Dane said, "I could use a weapon," and they advanced down the steps, Dane taking an AK-47 and ammo belt off one of the troopers.

McConn led the way out of the building. They broke left and ran for cover. Nina and Stone continued popping off bursts of rounds, keeping troopers down, some of them returning fire but none of the shots striking home.

McConn found Nina behind a stump. She whistled to Stone and the four started running through the growth, swatting branches and other obstacles aside.

Shooting behind them nicked at their former hiding space. Dane stopped long enough to look back and trigger a blind burst. Lights around the camp were snapping on again. Back-up generator.

"They'll be organized in a few minutes," he said, running with his friends again.

They reached a gulley and dropped into it.

"If they spread around the island chasing us, that

leaves Graypoole exposed," Nina said. "He's not the type to join the hunt."

Nina reloaded her weapon. "Here they come."

Dane looked where Nina pointed. They dropped low. Dane couldn't see the approaching figures as well as the others, but their movement was unmistakable.

Nina sank as low as she could. Dane kept his eyes forward. One of the troopers exposed too much of his upper body. Dane fired. The round hit the man's chest dead center. The other two opened up, shifting their bursts, the stingers from their automatic rifles ripping into trees and brush, geysering the dirt around their position. He fired at the next trooper as McConn and Stone started shooting too. Dane missed. The gunner rolled to better cover.

Nina crawled out of the dip and moved off to Dane's left, staying low as she ran between the trees.

"Damnit, Nina!"

One of the gunmen saw her and swung the M-4 her way.

"Nina down!"

Dane's AK spat flame. The trooper's head snapped back, painting a nearby tree with specks of red.

More shots from the troopers split the air overhead, the slugs singing like bees. Dane put his face into the dirt as McConn and Stone alternated bursts. Somebody on the other side screamed.

"More coming," McConn said.

Dane looked in the direction Nina had gone. Where was she?

CHAPTER 44

Nina peered through brush at the troopers fifteen yards away. She wanted to be closer than she was now. The closer she could get, the better chance of wiping them out the first time.

She broke from cover, closed the gap between her and the nearest trooper, swinging the butt of her rifle to connect with his head. He landed hard, his two buddies snapping their heads around. Nina's M-4 hammered against her shoulder as she riddled both men with slugs. When the rifle clicked empty, she popped out the magazine and replaced it with a spare. Staying low, Nina scanned for more. The crackle of weapons filled the night, boots stomping through the foliage, shouts here and there. She advanced, dropping and rolling every few feet, dirt flying each time she hit the ground. A large tree lay ahead. She ran to it, bracing against the rough trunk. A lone gunner, focused on where Dane, McConn and Stone were, didn't see her. She stroked the trigger and flame flashed from the M-4.

The burst stitched up the gunner's back to his head, which popped like a crushed watermelon. The man hit the ground.

The shouting grew louder and she looked back. More troopers closing in. Her throat felt suddenly dry as she realized the true odds they faced. They couldn't hold them off forever.

She cut across the battlefield and back to the gulley.

"Are you out of your mind?"

"More coming," Nina said as she settled beside Dane.

"I see them," Stone said.

"We can't stay here," McConn said. "I'm down to my last mag."

"Dev?"

"Two more."

"The dead have plenty of ammo," Nina said.

"We're not in a position for a shopping spree."

Dane held up a hand for everybody to stop talking, then made a downward gesture. They slid under as much of the foliage as they could. The troopers moved quickly, a leader shouting commands. He wanted to split the team three ways and directed them so. He led his group straight toward the gulley. Dane watched him through a gap in the leaves. If the troopers walked by, and they could hide until they were well inland, then going back for Graypoole wouldn't be so bad. Not ideal, but not certain death, either.

And that last Bell helicopter was calling his name.

The squad leader guided his team around the gulley but they still marched dreadfully close, and presently continued on their way, not bothering to stay quiet. They cut and slashed at anything in front of them, only the two in the rear really paying attention and keeping their rifles at the ready.

Dane and his crew waiting for at least a half hour, letting nature settle around them. Activity at the command center, once the generator put the lights back on, seemed quiet. Had every available man gone searching for them?

Dane started to move, the others following and they spread out in a line. They stopped at the dead bodies to help themselves to rifles and ammunition, all they could carry and started for the buildings. At the edge of the forest, Dane looked around.

There were a few troopers behind, two near the helicopter, two in front of the control center. But it was the bungalow that Dane focused on. Graypoole and the Iranian were still there, armed, with a trooper on the balcony as well.

Dane gestured for everybody to gather around and they made a plan.

Presently McConn broke off and worked his way closer to the helicopter. He waited.

Stone approached the control center.

Dane and Nina eyed the bungalow.

Dane freed the pin from a grenade and aimed for the control building, executing a perfect overhand toss. The grenade landed at the feet of the troopers there, exploding before they could react. The blast shook the ground and sent a ball of flame skyward.

McConn opened fire on the troopers near the chopper, cutting them down. One of his rounds cracked a window on the side of the helicopter.

Dane and Nina broke cover and ran for the bungalow.

Stone kicked in the door of the control room, tossing another grenade. He jumped out of the doorway. The blast filled the room. Swinging back inside, he opened fire on anybody still standing. Bodies not the ground fell over as the slugs ripped open their flesh.

Graypoole, Rostami the Iranian lawyer and the other

trooper braced themselves on the railing, firing on Dane and Nina. The slugs kicked up dirt around them. Dane dropped and rolled, stopping near a Jeep, and fired over the hood. The trooper's chest exploded and chunks of bloody mush splattered on Graypoole's suit. He didn't seem to notice. Nina continued running, gaining the foliage on the other side, starting her climb toward the stilts.

Dane tossed another grenade that sailed past the bungalow and detonated behind it, but the blast was enough to make Graypoole scream. The Iranian kept his aim on Dane, a salvo of shots tearing into the hood of the Jeep and shattering the glass. Nina triggered a burst that stitched through the deck floor but missed the Iranian, who then shifted his position and returned fire.

Dane ran forward, charging up the slope, firing as he moved. The AK-47 clicked empty. He dropped and rolled into the foliage, changing magazines as Nina returned fire. Dane rose and a shot split the air above his head. Graypoole adjusted his aim. Dane rolled as the second round punched into the ground where he'd been.

Dane stayed low and crawled through the foliage like a burrowing tick.

Dane stopped when he reached Nina. "I'm going around to the front."

"I'll cover you."

Dane pushed through the foliage with Nina's rifle hammering behind him. He scooted under the deck and crawled through the dirt beneath the house, stopping when the floor became too low, turning to crawl out on the side. He stayed low, avoiding the covered windows and circled around to the porch. More gunfire from the opposite side hid the sounds of him running to the porch and kicking in the door. He somersaulted through the entry way and came up on one knee.

Graypoole and the Iranian turned from the balcony at the same time. The Iranian's rifle came up as Dane fired, the muzzle flash filling the room. The Iranian took the salvo high in the chest and screamed as he tumbled over the railing to the slope below. Dane shifted to Graypoole, who dived to one side. Dane's weapon spat a burst and stopped, the weapon clicking empty. Dane tossed it aside and jumped to his left and Graypoole ran at him with flame spitting from the end of his gun.

Dane landed on the other side of a couch, falling between the narrow space between the couch and coffee table as bullets chewed through, filling the air with stuffing. Dane shoved himself forward along the carpet, turning over a chair, trying to get as far as he could. Then Graypoole's weapons stopped. Dane looked back. Graypoole worked the bolt of his gun, ejecting a jammed round and as he forced the bolt forward to fire again Dane drew his automatic and fired once. The shot nicked Graypoole's ear, who then threw the rifle straight at Dane. Dane dropped and covered the back of his head, the rifle slamming into the wall behind and when he looked back Graypoole was yelling, his face red with rage, flying over the couch with both hands open and ready for Dane's neck.

Dane grabbed the chair he'd tossed aside and lifted it between him and Graypoole, crashing the wood into the side of Graypoole's head. He landed on Dane anyway, breaking part of the chair, bumping into the coffee table as he came to rest, almost pinning Dane in place. Graypoole pushed up and pulled his right hand back, hammering Dane twice in the face. Dane grabbed a broken chair leg and smashed Graypoole in the side of the face. Dane shoved a knee between them and pushed, heaving Graypoole against the table once again before rolling out of the way, the debris from the chair gouging into his body.

Dane jumped to his feet same as Graypoole, who lashed out with a long roundhouse kick. Dane dropped, the other man's foot swishing overhead, but he didn't avoid the follow-up kick, which connected squarely with Dane's chest and propelled him back into the wall. The bungalow shook. Dane's breath left him, his vision spinning, but Graypoole was closing in for another strike. Dane deflected Graypoole's sharp jabs and punches, landing his own kick on Graypoole's left knee. Graypoole screamed, Dane lashing out with his own series of punches, driving the other man back. A roundhouse from Dane put Graypoole on the carpet. He rolled a few times, gaining some distance. Dane took out his fighting knife, holding the blade down, and advanced.

Graypoole jumped to his feet, his hands up defensively, making a slow circle as Dane neared with the knife. Dane closed the gap, raising the blade and stabbing downward, slicing open Graypoole's right arm and bringing the blade back for a swipe at his throat. Graypoole blocked the thrust, stepping back and as Dane lunged again Graypoole spun a kick right at Dane's hand. A snap filled the room, Dane crying out as the knife went flying and sunk an inch into the wall behind him. Another kick—breath left Dane as he doubled over from the strike to his middle. He landed on the carpet, rolling, sweat dripping into his eyes. He wiped his eyes, still unable to breath and Graypoole yanked the knife from the wall and came at Dane ferociously, landing with a knee in his groin, Dane throwing his arms up to block Graypoole, who raised the knife over his head. He plunged the blade down, Dane grabbing Graypoole's wrist and holding tight. He still couldn't breathe, felt his head throb and swell and Graypoole's strength didn't fade. The blade inched closer, aimed for Dane's left eye. He twisted his torso left, right, but Graypoole wouldn't budge. The blade descended some more, Graypoole's hot breath brushing Dane's nostrils. Rage still filled the man's eyes.

Another inch as Grypoole pushed harder.

Dane wedged his right knee between them. With the knee in place, Dane rolled left, the two men still locked together, Dane forcing a roll that put Graypoole under him. Dane straddled Graypoole this time, but Graypoole still had the knife and thrust it toward Dane's neck. Dane blocked Graypoole's arm. A vision filled Dane's mind. *Young girl. Brown eyes. It ends now!* Dane grabbed Graypoole's wrist, bending it back with as much force as he could muster. Graypoole screamed. His grip on the hilt loosened. Dane snatched the knife and plunged the blade into Graypoole's neck, pinning him to the floor beneath. Graypoole's mouth opened to scream, but with his throat run through, only a gush of blood appeared, the wanna-be terrorist quickly choking, his body thrashing. By the time Dane rose to his feet and caught his breath, Graypoole had not only stopped making noises, he stopped moving entirely.

His sightless eyes remained open.

Somebody entered the room. Dane turned. Nina stood in the doorway holding her Kalashnikov. "Is he dead?"

Dane spat on Graypoole's body. "He's dead."

"Then let's go home, lover."

CHAPTER 45

◆━━━━◆

Dane and Nina bolted down the slope and back across the grounds to the chopper, Dane with a fresh rifle collected from Graypoole's dead Iranian friend.

McConn sat in the pilot's seat, Stone outside the cabin on guard. He yelled for them to run faster as he swung his weapon toward a returning force only he could see. His rifle spoke as he shifted his aim, yelling louder for Dane and Nina to hurry.

Slugs smacked the dirt around them, whistled through the air. Dane kept his eyes on the chopper, Nina to his right, shielded by him from the incoming fire.

They reached the chopper. Dane pivoted to face the enemy, blocking Nina and Stone from their fire and triggered a pair of salvos to keep the troopers back. Nina yelled his name. Dane turned and jumped aboard, bumping into Nina as he settled in the cabin. Nina leaned in and kissed him on the cheek.

"You're welcome," he said. She smiled.

Stone slammed the cabin door shut as McConn worked the stick and raised the chopper off the platform. Stray slugs nicked at the landing skids and thumped into the body. McConn steered toward the ocean and put the battleground behind them.

Dane, Nina and Stone sat back against the cabin walls, gasping, tossing weapons aside and tearing off their gear.

"What's next?" Nina said.

"Breakfast in Barcelona is a good idea," Dane said.

The chopper flew over the ocean and into the night.

Dane and Lukavina sat in a quiet neighborhood park in D.C., kids playing behind them, a hot dog vendor across the way. Cars rumbled by.

"You don't look very happy," the CIA man said. The shade of a tree covered them from the bright sun.

"I'm not." Dane, arms folded, wearing a new suit, couldn't shake his frown. His right sleeve was creeping up too far. He unfolded his arms and pulled the sleeve back into place.

"We couldn't send help."

"I understand that. It's the least of what I'm upset about."

"What then?"

"I don't think we won anything," Dane said. "We were behind the eight ball the whole time. How many people died in San Francisco and Seattle? Derya Teke is still at large. This wasn't a victory. By any means."

Lukavina didn't answer right away. Then: "We got even."

"That's not enough for me."

"It's all I have to offer."

"What happened to our FBI contact in Seattle? O'Brien was his name."

Lukavina shook his head.

Dane sighed. "Always." He stood up and Lukavina followed. Dane held out his hand. They shook. "Until next time," Dane said.

"So long," Lukavina said.

Dane crossed the grass and rejoined Nina, McConn and Stone, who waited in an SUV parked on the curb. He climbed into the front seat.

"Anybody ever been to Goa?" McConn said from the back seat. "I hear it's nice this time of year."

"India?" Dane said.

"Yup. Right on the coast."

"What's in Goa?"

"More like *who* is in Goa. I found our loose end last night. Thought you might like to know about him."

Dane did indeed.

Waves crashed on the beach. Behind a wall about one hundred yards from the water sat a single-story home full of lights, music, and laughter.

The party ran well into the night, finally ending around four a.m., and that's when a tipsy Derya Teke staggered into his dark bedroom. He wasn't alone. He collided with a wall and his female companion laughed.

"Careful," Teke said, "that painting is worth two million dollars."

"Oooohhhhh," the girl said.

Another thud. This time Teke laughed. When he finally found the light switch, the first thing they saw was the bed.

The second thing was the man sitting in a corner chair. A window leading to a back patio was open a crack, letting in the crisp ocean air.

The girl screamed.

Steve Dane raised the Colt Gold Cup and said, "The girl can leave."

Suddenly sober, the woman bolted from the room.

Teke remained behind on unsteady legs, his hands out on either side.

Dane fired once. The crack of the shot filled the room and Derya Teke fell forward, a pool of blood quickly soaking into the carpet. Dane left the chair, stood over the man's body and fired another shot into his head.

Maybe getting even wasn't so bad after all.

Dane put the gun away and slipped out the door.

Hopping the wall opposite the beach, Dane landed on pavement and headed for the curb where a car sat, engine running, Nina behind the wheel. He climbed in and smiled at her. She put the car in gear and drove away.

"Next time," she said, "you wait with the car."

Dane grinned. "Yes, dear."

San Francisco

He insisted on going back.

Nina had tried to talk him out of it, but Dane stated clearly that he was not going to change his mind.

She hung back near a cluster of headstones while Dane approached the twin stones of Lilly Klove and her father, James. He held a single red rose. Nina figured he wanted to be alone. It was none of her business what he might say, if he said anything, but he somehow needed the closure. She understood that much. If he truly kept seeing the girl's face in his mind's eye, maybe a visit to her grave would put an end to the vision.

Dane bent down and placed the rose in front of the girl's headstone. He stood back, hands locked in front of him and contemplated the stone a moment. Nina breathed quietly, waiting. She hoped Dane found what he was looking for but doubted he would. He'd spend the rest of his life looking for *it*, whatever *it* was, and all she knew for sure was that she'd be by his side the whole time. No matter what happened. No matter how long the journey lasted.

Presently he turned and walked back to her. He wasn't smiling, but his face showed peaceful content. A weight was gone from his shoulders.

Maybe that was enough for now.

She smiled when he took her hand.

A LOOK AT: THE TERMINATION PROTOCOL (SCOTT STILETTO BOOK 1)

◼━━◼

The Termination Protocol is the first book in the hard-edged, action thriller series — Scott Stiletto.

The United States is under siege, and the enemy has help from the White House!

Scott Stiletto is one of the CIA's toughest assets, a veteran of numerous missions, an operative with compassion and ruthlessness in equal parts.

His enemy is the New World Revolutionary Front, a terrorist organization seeking to overthrow the government of the United States and install their own puppet—a willing puppet, who is already very close to the president he wishes to replace.

With freedom and justice hanging in the balance, Scott Stiletto gives no quarter. He will give the enemy a one-way ticket to hell!

"...99% pure action fun, no additives. I had to stop reading the book several times just to catch my breath..." — Ian Kharitonov

AVAILABLE NOW ON AMAZON

ABOUT THE AUTHOR

A twenty-five year veteran of radio and television broadcasting, Brian Drake has spent his career in San Francisco where he's filled writing, producing, and reporting duties with stations such as KPIX-TV, KCBS, KQED, among many others. Currently carrying out sports and traffic reporting duties for Bloomberg 960, Brian Drake spends time between reports and carefully guarded morning and evening hours cranking out action/adventure tales. A love of reading when he was younger inspired him to create his own stories, and he sold his first short story, "The Desperate Minutes," to an obscure webzine when he was 25 (more years ago than he cares to remember, so don't ask). Many more short story sales followed before he expanded to novels, entering the self-publishing field in 2010, and quickly building enough of a following to attract the attention of several publishers and other writing professionals. Brian Drake lives in California with his wife and two cats, and when he's not writing he is usually blasting along the back roads in his Corvette with his wife telling him not to drive so fast, but the engine is so loud he usually can't hear her.

You will find him regularly blogging at www.briandrake88.blogspot.com